Tot...

...ro Fair and the Beast

Anywhere and Always
Falling for the Tycoon
Snowbound with the Billionaire

Minne-sorta Falling in Love
Semper Fitz

Minne-sorta Falling in Love

SEMPER FITZ

AURORA RUSSELL

Semper Fitz
ISBN # 978-1-83943-766-3
©Copyright Aurora Russell 2022
Cover Art by Kelly Martin ©Copyright January 2022
Interior text design by Claire Siemaszkiewicz
Totally Bound Publishing

SEMPER FITZ

Dedication

First and foremost, this book is a love letter to Minnesota. From Paul Bunyan to population signs, "duck, duck, gray duck" to The Mall, it's a magical place. I hope this story takes all who read it "Up to the Lake." Also, to all those who serve or have served in the armed forces, including those close to me, I am in awe of your dedication, bravery and sacrifice.

To my own gruff hero and our two mini-hellions, you guys inspire and humble me every day. To my dad and stepmom, your support means the world to me...truly. To my brother and sister-in-law and your growing family, thank you for your unwavering love and friendship. To my close friends, thank you guys from the bottom of my heart for always making me smile, filling my soul to the brim with a mix of joy and pure silliness. And yes, I promise one of my next books will have a sexy Highlander. I also want to thank the rest of my wonderful family, including my in-laws, because you all are just awesome. Last, but most definitely not least, thank you to my fantastic publisher, Totally Bound, and editor, Jamie Rose, for believing in me.

Chapter One

Clara Olafson hummed a little to herself as she walked heavily down the overgrown trail. This far out into the forest, the trails weren't maintained as regularly as the ones closer to the visitor center. The morning air was crisp—northern Minnesota in late August could feel like October or November in the rest of the country—but she liked it that way. The cool air buffeting her felt like a familiar, albeit chilly, blanket. Like *home*. Plus, it quickened her steps, which was good for her and the baby. A couple of times lately, she'd had the oddest sensation, almost like a trickle of ice-water down her spine, that she was being watched or followed, but she blamed the crazy pregnancy hormonal imbalance. This morning, though, she felt nothing but the fresh breeze behind her.

She'd started the habit of an early-morning walk when she'd moved out to the cabin two months earlier, and she intended to keep it up until the day she went into labor—which actually could be pretty soon. The OB she'd been seeing in St. Paul—*before*—had said to stay active, and she wanted to do everything she could to make sure that the little life she carried had the best possible start. She'd read several books, along with what felt like a couple of thousand websites, and she was avoiding lunchmeat, green tea, fake sweeteners, caffeine—even chocolate. Goodness, chocolate had been the hardest to give up, with coffee a close second. She now had a recurring dream where she walked into a dimly lit coffee house and ordered a massive frozen-mocha-latte-smoothie with curls of dark chocolate and mounds of whipped cream on top, but she always woke up before she could take a sip. Her mouth watered just thinking about it.

"No," she chided, half speaking to herself and also to the baby. "No chocolate for the baby, no matter how much Mama wants it." She reached down to rub her swollen belly, as she did so often these days, and smiled at the firm kick she got in response, right under her palm. A rush of affection and protectiveness so intense that it almost frightened her swept through, taking her by surprise. It was amazing to hold a tiny, growing human inside her, but also terrifying to be so totally and solely responsible for someone else.

Even in the midst of her awe, the craving persisted, so intense that she could almost taste the chocolate melting on her tongue. *Maybe I'm just longing for something sweet?* She wasn't supposed to have too much sugar, but fruit was definitely still okay. The berries on the blackberry and raspberry bushes a little farther down the path were just starting to ripen again. They would be tart and juicy. She licked her lips at the thought and smiled at her own eagerness. *Anyone who gets between a pregnant woman and her desired food deserves whatever happens to him.* She quickened her pace, thankful she'd worn long pants and sleeves to avoid the prickly bushes. If there were enough berries, maybe she'd even come back later with a pail and pick enough for a pie. *Oh, good Lord*, the idea of a piece of pie, even just a tiny sliver, warm from the oven with a flaky crust, was so wonderful that she almost groaned aloud.

Practically trotting and out of breath by the time she reached the bushes, she was thrilled to see a few ripe berries straight away, which she snapped off their thin branches and popped into her mouth. Cold juice exploded on her tongue, and she sighed with pleasure. The ripe berries were few and far between, though. Most of them were still hard and green. Even so, there were enough on each bush to take her deep into the thicket as she sought out every last berry that was ready to eat, crunching them with gusto. It could have been some crazy sensory thing, but she didn't know if she'd ever tasted anything more delicious.

At first, she thought the moaning might be coming from her stomach. Heaven knew it made all sorts of noises these days—gurgles, churns and growls so loud they woke her up at night. But this sound was too loud and too deep. She froze and tilted her head, listening. When the low moan came again, her heart seemed to jump right up into her throat. *What the heck?* Taking a slow, calming breath and narrowing her eyes, she scanned the thicket. *Probably a deer in distress*, she reassured herself. At least she hoped it was a deer, because if it were a moose or a bear, she could be in real trouble. She couldn't make out much of anything through the thick leaf-cover at first, but finally a slight shaking in the bushes ahead and to her right signaled the location of whatever injured creature was there.

She hesitated. A prudent woman would go back to the cabin and call for help. She knew this. She *should* be careful and not her usual impulsive self. But then the noise came again, so sad and filled with pain that it made her throat tighten and her eyes fill with tears. Pure, uncontrollable sympathy made her step one foot forward, and her distinctly *un*-prudent decision was made. *If the animal can make a noise like that,* she reasoned, *it's unlikely to be able to move enough to hurt me if I stay back. And I won't get too close.*

The stand of bushes was situated in a small valley with steep inclines that were blanketed with pine trees rising high on either side. As she got nearer to the wounded creature, she could see a faint trail of crushed and broken foliage leading to it from the opposite direction, and she guessed that the poor animal had probably fallen from the higher ground. Her heart squeezed with compassion. *It must be in so much pain.* She slowed her steps, carefully placing her weight on the balls of her feet instead of the heels and trying to breathe silently to avoid startling the mystery animal.

She braced herself for a very ugly scene, but what she found instead made her suck in a surprised breath. Two huge, black boots stood out dark against the green undergrowth, and her eyes followed their forms to two blue-jeans-clad legs, one of which looked somewhat twisted. Her gaze trailed up farther, to where the form was more obscured by leaves, but she could still make out an enormous hand and the weave of a thick green sweater, shifting slightly with the man's breathing. She hurried forward.

"Oh, my goodness, you poor man! Where's the worst pain?" she asked, trying to keep her voice quiet so as not to startle him. There was no answer, apart from another piteous groan, and when his face finally came into full view, she saw why. His eyes were closed, and an ugly lump had formed at his temple, already dark with a hint of the bad bruising to come. The blow must have also knocked him unconscious.

She lowered herself to the ground awkwardly, her movements hampered by the clumsiness of late-pregnancy and the ever-present swelling that made her fingers and toes feel like little sausages stuffed into casings that were too small. She wanted to assess where his injuries might be, though, and to do that, she needed to get closer. She'd taken several first-aid classes as a young teenager, practically a requirement as a doctor's daughter in a rural area, so she felt reasonably optimistic she could stabilize the worst of whatever his injuries were before she ran back to the cabin to call 9-1-1. *Why in the world did I choose today of all days not to bring my cell phone?* She cursed under her breath, immediately murmuring an apology to her baby.

As her movements brought her closer to him, she couldn't help but notice that, apart from his injuries, the man appeared to be in extremely good shape. His leg muscles bulged, even through the thick denim of his jeans, and his broad shoulders and chest looked solid and strong. She glanced at his face, noticing that his hair was cropped close to his skull — *the length a lot of military and ex-military men keep it*, she thought absently. Even if she couldn't see his eyes, he was undeniably handsome with high cheekbones, dark brows and eyelashes, a strong chin and nose, and soft-looking lips. He was younger than she'd initially thought, too. *Maybe in his early thirties.*

Running carefully light hands over his legs, she felt the spot where one of his knees was twisted and swollen, but she was relieved that she didn't feel anything else that seemed out of place on his lower extremities. There were a few areas that were uneven, but she guessed it could be fabric bunching or debris from the fall. She skimmed her fingers over his hips to his chest, which were just as hard and muscular as she'd guessed, to his bulky arms. To her dismay, one of his wrists also felt slightly enlarged. Finally, she moved a tentative hand to his head. She rose onto her knees, leaning over for a better view to see how large and swollen the area was, which should be pretty visible through his ultra-short hair. Head wounds could be tricky, bleeding internally as well as externally. The swelling there was almost certainly what was causing his unconsciousness.

Just as the tips of her fingers made contact with the most swollen spot, without a breath of warning one of the man's mammoth hands clamped around her wrist, stopping her from moving. She squeaked and tried to take her arm away, but his grip held her firm. When her gaze flashed to his face, he was staring back at her with bright blue eyes that were filled with a mix of suspicion and confusion.

Colin Fitzhugh swam in a sea of agony. He was hot—it was always so hot in this damn desert—and disoriented. At first the light touch on his legs had made him tense, thinking it was someone looking to loot his body. The joke was on them, then, because he wasn't dead, although with the way he felt, he might wish he were. Had he been burning in a fire? Or was that before?

He tensed to rise up and strike, but the hands continued with aching gentleness. Not seeking or prodding his pockets but feeling...*like a medic*. He tried to pry his eyes open through the gritty sand that never seemed to leave them entirely, but they refused. He felt light fingers on his arms and chest. When they moved to his temple, though, his head began to throb and pulse with a bright, white-hot pain. He grabbed for the hand almost reflexively.

The sight that met his surprised gaze was most…unexpected. Instead of the fatigue-covered, helmeted medic he'd imagined, he saw an angel. Well, as close to an angel as he'd ever seen. With pale, creamy skin, pink cheeks and lips, and large hazel eyes fringed with thick reddish lashes, and with her face framed by fuzzy curls that had escaped her ponytail, the strange woman looked as compassionate as she was beautiful. Her expression was cautious, with a wrinkle of concern appearing between her eyebrows, but also kind. When she tried to move away and his grip stopped her, instead of becoming frantic, she went still, almost as if she were preparing to soothe a wild animal.

Come to think of it, maybe he was like a wild animal. She certainly wasn't wrong to be wary. And where the hell *was* he? It didn't feel like the desert, though his lips and throat sure as hell were parched.

"Whe…?" He tried to say more, but his voice, or the gravelly croak that passed for his voice right now, cracked and died.

The woman seemed to understand, though, and her face was gentle and sympathetic. "In the woods near Cameronville. It's Thursday, around six-thirty in the morning. You seem to be hurt pretty badly, and I'm guessing it was in a fall. Do you remember how long you've been out here?"

Cameronville. His mind seized on the name of the town near the state park where he'd come to escape, and memories came flooding back. The assault was almost physically painful, or maybe that was just his injuries starting to throb as the blood rushed through them. His *latest* injuries, rather, because now that he

13

could remember more clearly, he knew that he was a man who had been severely wounded before, in ways that made this seem almost insignificant.

It was ironic, really, that the profession he'd chosen to prove to himself and his family that he could make it on his own, without the Fitzhugh fortune or influence, had turned around and bitten him on the ass. The Corps—his last mission in particular—had ended up taking more from him than he'd known he had to give.

"Oh shoot, is your throat hurting? Or can you not remember?" The woman's voice was low and clear, and her concern sounded genuine. To his horror, his eyes stung with unexpected tears. Apparently, he had become unaccustomed to gentleness.

To distract himself from that uncomfortable realization, he studied her face again. The kindness she had shown to approach a near-stranger and drop down to the rocky ground, covered in thorny underbrush, touched something in his chest that hadn't stirred in a long time. But it hadn't been smart of her, out here alone in the woods, to come so close to a strange man. Even injured he knew of at least six ways he could hurt and incapacitate her if she were an enemy. Embarrassed when he realized he still held her small wrist in a vise-like grip, he dropped it as if it had burned him. He hated the sick feeling that churned in the depths of his stomach when she started to rub her wrist as if he might've hurt her.

"So sorry," he managed in a scratchy whisper. He expected her to move away immediately now that she was free of him, but instead she leaned closer—so close he could see that something had slightly stained her lips—*berry juice?*

"It's all right. I expect I startled you. Maybe I'm the one who should be sorry for taking you by surprise, only I just couldn't tell how badly you were injured without touching you," she said apologetically.

He could hardly trust what he was hearing, to believe she was truly that sweet. Searching her face for signs of subterfuge, all he found was earnest openness. When he opened his mouth to answer, his poor, abused throat refused to produce any sound — and it hurt like a son of a bitch, like he'd swallowed razors with his thermos of coffee. His throat had never quite been the same after the fire, though.

"Since your vocal cords don't seem to be cooperating, how about I guess and you just nod?" she suggested tactfully.

He signaled his agreement. It made sense.

"Did you fall overnight in the dark?" The sympathy in her eyes bled into her tone as well.

He shook his head no, remembering that the gray pre-dawn light had just been melting into pretty pink, gold and orange when he'd lost his footing like the greenest recruit.

The woman smiled encouragingly. "That's good. I'm glad you weren't out here in the dark. So, it was sometime this morning, then?"

He nodded his assent.

She cocked her head to one side, considering. He couldn't help but notice that she had an elegant neck and a pretty, healthy curve to her cheek. "That would make it sometime within the past fifteen minutes, so that's really good. The paramedics will want to know you were unconscious for under half an hour."

Paramedics. God, no. His arms and legs went rigid as his mind threw him into a near panic. Paramedics meant hospitals, and every cell, every fiber of his being revolted at the idea of another hospital. Maybe someday he'd be able to enter one again, but not now, so soon after leaving the hellhole he'd been trapped in for months — and probably never again as a patient. He thought he'd rather die. When she moved as if to rise, he stretched an arm to her shoulder, keeping his touch light this time.

She stilled and turned the full force of her clear gaze at him, apologetic again. "I'm so sorry to have to leave for a bit to call for help, but my cabin isn't far. Like a dope, I didn't bring my cell phone on my walk this morning. But I promise I'll be back to wait with you for the ambulance."

His stomach twisted and he felt physically ill at the idea of the ambulance, with its antiseptic smells and well-meaning attendants. The jerk he gave his head made it throb so hard that he thought she might be able to see the blood pulsing at his temples. "No," he ground out painfully, "*please.*" His voice cracked and gave out again.

"No ambulance?" she guessed. He nodded, his relief almost palpable.

She frowned and the little line appeared between her brows again. "Well, I suppose I can drive you to the hospital myself if we can manage to get back to my cabin. I really don't want to move you, though, in case you have a spine injury."

He shook his head again and the throbbing beat like an echo, bruising him from the inside out.

"No hospital either?" she said, looking wary.

He gave a tight nod, really just an incline of his head. The headache was intense and his movement was only making it worse, but at least now she understood.

The woman pursed her lips, which made them look full and pink...kissable. *Where the hell did that thought come from?* He didn't have time to dwell on it as she spoke again.

"You're not...some kind of criminal, are you? Although I guess you'd be a pretty crummy criminal if you told me, wouldn't you?" She gave a wry laugh, and Fitz was surprised into a small answering smile.

He shook his head again, wincing even as he did so, and tried to speak but just ended up whispering the words, "No, not a criminal."

Where before her gaze had been concerned but trusting, now it was suspicious and hesitant. Fitz hated that he'd put that suspicion there. He racked his brain for an idea of how to explain without speaking, then it hit him. It was so simple that it was silly.

Shuddering, he rolled to one side, feeling as if he were being stabbed by a thousand knives all at once.

"Don't move! What—?" The woman started to speak but her question broke off in a gasp when he lifted his sweater and undershirt to expose his chest.

He didn't look at her face. He didn't want to see her reaction if it was horror, sympathy or disgust, all the reactions he'd become accustomed to in the last six months—but he knew what she would see. His USMC tattoo on his torso was the last smooth skin above the mess of scars that covered him from his chest all the way down to his foot on his left side. The skin was red and angry in spots, shiny and lighter in others, since the rate of healing from multiple skin grafts had varied. He had been pieced and sewn back together like Frankenstein's monster. He hated for anyone to see this part of him and had taken to keeping it covered up, but he'd had to make her trust him.

Her silence felt like it stretched an eternity, though it was probably only a couple of seconds. He had the fleeting thought that all the other guys in prep school who hadn't been quite as wealthy or popular as the devil-may-care younger Fitzhugh boy would love to see him now, scarred and dirty on the ground.

"No hospital," she agreed at last, her voice sounding tight.

Keeping his face averted, he pulled his T-shirt and thick sweater back down and began the painful process of struggling to his feet.

Chapter Two

Clara was amazed at the stranger's strength and stoicism. The injuries to his head, knee and wrist had to be agonizing. She could only guess at the aches and suffering that his older injuries—though they didn't look all that old—must have caused and might still cause him. Yet he managed to sit up then rise to his knees, grunting as the swollen knee connected with the rough forest floor. She hated that he was moving at all, but if he was determined to stand up, she would help him. And he did seem totally alert, even if he was gruff from his injuries. She scrambled to an awkward crouch as well and sidled up next to him. He was so tall that, stooping a bit, she realized she only came up to his shoulder and could probably fit right under his arm.

Without thinking closely about what she was going to do, she ducked under one massive, muscular shoulder and wrapped her arm gently around his thick torso. As much as she could reach, anyway. It was like hugging an old-growth pine trunk. He huffed in a surprised breath, and when she looked up, she saw shock flash in his eyes, but it was quickly replaced by pain and determination. *Maybe a little gratitude, too.* He didn't push her away, although she could sense that he wished he didn't need help.

The position was oddly intimate, and the feeling of his hard muscles and warmth pressed all along her side made something tingle and sizzle painfully to life within her. He smelled dark and masculine, somehow exotic, and her nose twitched with appreciation. Then she scolded herself. The poor man was badly wounded and had obviously been through a great deal. What the heck was she thinking, ogling him like she was? And why had her body chosen this exact moment, after months and months of having zero interest whatsoever in the opposite sex, to come suddenly back to life? She shook her head and concentrated on being a steady column of support for the soldier to lean on as he tried to get to his feet.

He trembled and there was a thin sheen of sweat that appeared on his forehead, which had gone very pale, as he shifted his uninjured leg so that his boot rested squarely on the ground. It left all his weight temporarily on his swollen knee on his left side, and she could see the muscles in his jaw clenching with what must be intense pain.

"You're almost there. How about we stand up on three?" she murmured encouragingly. He inclined his head tersely and she could see little lines of strain bracketing his mouth, making him look older and more vulnerable all of a sudden.

"One…two…*three*," she counted quickly, then they rose as one, surging upward. She felt him lean heavily on her, so heavily that it hurt her shoulders, but she didn't mind. The most important thing was getting him back to her cabin as fast as possible. Her heart had just about cracked when he'd shown her his scarred chest as he'd looked away. She ached for the torture that he must have suffered to have those scars and for what it must have cost him to reveal it to a total stranger.

Finally, he was on his feet, with her still tucked under his arm. The sound of their heavy breathing was loud in the quiet of the chilly morning. Relief flooded her body that he was all right enough to stand, and she wouldn't have to drag him. Even the baby gave a little kick of appreciation.

"It's not too far, maybe only a quarter of a mile, but let me know if you want to rest." Clara hadn't really expected him to agree but was surprised at the vehemence of his refusal as he shook his head fiercely and grunted what could have been a *hell, no.*

"All right. Head 'em up, move 'em out," she agreed in a light tone, but he looked to be concentrating too hard to react.

The first section of their walk was the worst, going back through the thick blackberry and raspberry bushes, and thorns scratched at her hands and a little at her cheeks, though the bulk of the soldier's arm protected her face for the most part. When they reached the path, the walking got easier, but her companion's breath grew more labored. She could practically feel his energy flagging as he leaned more and more heavily on her, and she thought that he must be fueled by pure grit and determination at this point, since he had to feel absolutely rotten.

When they rounded the bend to the path leading to her family's little cabin, she felt like cheering. The stranger's steps were becoming leaden, making him stumble with increasing frequency. She couldn't wait to get him settled on the large guest bed before he collapsed, as she feared he might if they had to go much farther. Thanking heaven that her brother had added a little ramp for their grandfather when Pop had started having trouble navigating the steps a few years earlier, she guided the soldier to the railing. He grabbed it so hard that his knuckles blanched almost instantly. He closed his eyes and held on, looking grim.

Clara hurried to the door, pulling out her keys with fingers that fumbled a little in her haste. They hadn't used to lock the door at all, but then some parkgoers had stolen all the drinks right out of the fridge the past year when she'd been up for a visit, and it had scared her enough that she always locked it now. Still, it was distinctly inconvenient to have an additional delay at the moment. Finally, the key slid into place, and she managed to swing the door open.

"Just a couple of more steps and we'll have you settled into a soft bed with something to drink," Clara assured the stranger as she bustled back to help guide him up the ramp. He looked pretty out of it, sweating and shaking, his eyes narrowed with strain, but he still seemed determined. If she hadn't believed he was a Marine before, she would have believed it now.

Somehow, they managed to make it through the house and into the guest bedroom, where he collapsed with a groan on top of the covers. Pausing only to make sure that he wouldn't fall off the bed, she hurried to the kitchen, pouring him a glass of water from one of the jugs in the fridge. The cabin didn't have any running water, so she filled jugs from the pump in the backyard and kept them cold. She started to return to him with just the glass but then turned back to the tiny kitchen, rummaging around in the silverware drawer until she found the neon-pink bendy straw she knew she still had from her best friend's last visit with her four-year-old daughter. Silly, but it would make it easier for the stranger to drink.

When she returned to the bedroom, the injured man hadn't moved, but he wasn't asleep, since he cracked his eyes open as she came to sit on the side of the bed. The old bedframe creaked ominously under the mattress at their combined weight. His piercing gaze focused on the glass of water she held, and he struggled to sit up a little more, propping himself up on forearms so toned that even through the weave of his sweater she could see the muscles rippling as he moved.

"Here... Let me help you," Clara said softly when it was clear he wasn't going to be able to hold the glass, and she moved toward him, leaning in to hold the straw to his lips. Again, she felt that same zing of awareness, as if all her cells were going onto high alert, as she got close enough to feel his warmth. His breath stirred the little wisps of hair around her face, tickling her cheeks.

He drank greedily, thirstily, sucking the entire glass of water down in almost no time. As if the movement had exhausted him, he lay back down heavily onto the pillows. Still, she thought he looked a little better. His face wasn't as sickly pale as it had gotten earlier.

"More?" she asked. His bright blue eyes caught hers and held for a long moment. His expression was...intense. Under the pain, she thought she saw thanks mixed with guardedness and maybe a tiny spark of awareness, but she thought she was likely imagining that to make herself feel better for getting hot and bothered over an injured soldier. *Ridiculous to think he's interested in a huge, pregnant stranger.* She felt her cheeks flush and she could tell that he noticed.

"*Please,*" he rasped.

Embarrassed by her totally transparent reactions to him, she stood up too fast and the room began to spin so that she had to put a hand out to steady herself on the wall. She rubbed her belly with her other hand, reassured by the answering kick that she felt from within. She took several long breaths until her balance and her bearings returned. "It's okay, baby. Stay calm," she whispered.

Fitz felt something he hadn't thought he'd feel again at his little rescuer's words. She spoke with such love and tenderness that he felt an answering sense of belonging and awareness that he'd thought he might no longer be able to feel — then reality broke over him like an icy wave. What the hell was his messed-up brain thinking? She didn't know him well enough to speak to him like that. In his current, strange situation, he might wish she had, but those words weren't meant for him. Something was wrong.

He studied her back as she faced away from him, realizing the hand she held on the wall was steadying her. "Are you all right?" he asked with concern, steeling himself against the soreness he would feel when he stood to help her.

When she turned back toward him, he noticed something he couldn't believe he'd missed. As he'd thought, she was still petite and curvy with fuzzy hair, kind eyes and an elegant neck. She also had a giant, rounded belly, denoting that she was in the very advanced stages of pregnancy.

"Oh my God, you're pregnant!" he exclaimed in a gravelly voice before he could stop his mouth from forming the words. "You're, wow, you're *really* pregnant." Instantly he regretted his observation. Apparently, he had been out of polite company for way too long, and could he *be* any more awkward and uncomfortable? His childhood nanny would have been aghast if she'd heard him.

The woman looked surprised at first and he waited for her to take offense, but instead a slow smile spread across her face until he could see that she had dimples on both of her cheeks. Her hazel eyes flashed and sparkled, and she looked utterly lovely. "Yep, definitely super pregnant," she agreed. "Eight months along, but it feels about like eighteen at this point."

"Sorry...I, ah, hadn't noticed earlier, so I was surprised. Didn't meant to offend you, ma'am," he stammered, unintentionally slipping back into a military cadence. His voice was still rough, although his throat did feel better after the water.

She smiled and waved her hand dismissively. "No problem. You were understandably thinking of other things. I'm totally not offended." She paused and smiled again. It was a beautiful smile. "Actually, it's sort of refreshing. No one else I've spoken to lately mentions anything *but* my pregnancy and the baby."

A smile tugged at Fitz's lips — and what was it about this woman that made him want to smile when he'd barely smiled at all in the past eight months? — but the smile died when he remembered that he'd put this woman and her baby in danger by insisting that she help him instead of calling for an ambulance. God, he'd practically begged her. His ears got warm, a sure sign of the shame he felt.

"Were you hurt when you helped me? I...well, I never would have allowed you to if I'd know about your, ah, condition." It was hard to get the words out around the guilt that threatened to rise up and choke him.

She surprised him again when she came closer to the bed and put a reassuring hand on top of his where it lay on the quilt that was underneath him. Her touch made something hot unfurl inside of his chest. "No, no, I'm fine! I just stood up too quickly. It's one of the dangers of being pregnant—along with about a billion others. I was happy to help you," she assured him, and her words smoothed the edges of the worst of his guilt.

"Still, it couldn't have been good to strain yourself, ma'am. I'm sorrier than I can ever say for forcing you," he answered gravely.

Her eyes flashed again, this time with spirit, and he realized his little savior had a temper. *It makes her even more delightful,* he thought, but squelched that thought immediately. A beautiful woman like her, eight months pregnant with child, surely had a large, loving man around—a man who wouldn't appreciate someone else getting ideas about his wife.

"Now let's get one thing straight. You *didn't* force me, and you *couldn't* force me to do anything I didn't want to—well, not without a heck of a fight, and I fight dirty. *I* found *you,* checked on you and agreed to bring you back here, knowing it would mean I'd have to help you. I'm pregnant, yeah, but that didn't affect my intelligence, and I know my limits." Her cheeks flushed a bright pink as she spoke, and her chest rose and fell with her temper.

"And another thing," she said, and he braced himself. "Stop calling me 'ma'am'. It makes me feel old. You can call me Clara."

He was torn between relief that, thank God, it really didn't seem to have hurt her to lug his sorry, wounded ass through the woods, and amusement at her indignation at being called 'ma'am'. His face, however, settled on amusement, and he didn't think he hid it well by the way she pursed her lips.

"Sorry, ma...I mean, uh, Clara." He cleared his throat uncomfortably. "All my friends call me Fitz. And I didn't mean to offend you...again," Fitz finished in his rough voice, feeling sheepish.

Clara—and he thought her name suited her perfectly—gave a small smile. "No apology necessary. I'm, well, a little...no, *a lot* touchy these days. Hormones. I was crying this morning when I noticed a hole in my favorite socks, for cripes' sake. So, I'm not really that offended. I just wanted to be clear."

She looked flustered so he nodded to let her know he understood.

"Now that we've cleared things up, let me get you that second glass of water, then I'll call Lars. Fair warning that he is a doctor, but I promise I'll make sure he doesn't take you to the hospital." Fitz watched her face as she spoke, and she looked totally honest. With deep surprise, he realized he trusted her. He believed her when she said he wouldn't be forced to go to the hospital. She didn't know who he was, really, so she couldn't be acting the way she was to get something from him. He inclined his head in a small nod of agreement and she went to the other room, returning quickly with another full glass of water, still with the ridiculous neon pink straw.

He felt steady enough to sit up and take the glass from her this time with the hand and wrist that hadn't been injured, drinking the water more slowly than before. Its chill felt good all over again on the rawness of his throat.

Clara returned to the other room, and he could hear her talking to someone on the phone, but her call was brief and she was back almost before he finished his water. She held out her hand and he handed her the glass, hating that even his good arm felt weak enough that he might not be able to hold it up for long.

"I caught him before he left for the clinic, so he should be here in about fifteen minutes," she said. "You do look like you've improved some, but since you were unconscious, I really think we'd better have him look at your head." She bit her full lower lip and the little crinkle reappeared in her forehead.

Fitz understood where she was coming from. And it couldn't hurt, since this doctor made house calls. He must be a friend or... Fitz didn't like the surge of unexpected envy that went through him at the thought that maybe Lars was her husband or boyfriend.

"Thank you," he answered. The next question popped out of his mouth almost of its own volition. "Is Lars excited about the baby?"

Clara looked at him a little oddly before answering. "Yeah, sure. Although he's pretty overprotective and hates that I'm alone out here so much."

"How often are you alone? And how *is* this place in the middle of the state park?" Fitz realized that he didn't much care for the idea of Clara out here by herself, either, even though he clearly didn't have that right. It was none of his business, and he should try to remember that.

"We're not technically in the state park. Our cabin was already here, so they carved out a little tongue of land that extends into the state park, just for my grandparents," she explained, answering his second question first. "And I'm alone out here pretty much all the time, although, of course, Lars checks on me every day. I don't know how he makes the time. A few of my friends come by too, when they can."

Fitz felt his temper rise much higher than it should have at the thought of this Lars leaving her alone for what sounded like the majority of every day when her pregnancy was so far along. Didn't the bastard realize what he had? "I know it's not my place, and maybe I'm old-fashioned, but I believe a man ought to be there for his woman, not just stop by because he's so busy." Fitz heard his voice deepening and roughening as he spoke, but he was really pissed.

Clara looked confused at first, but then understanding crept into her eyes. "You're right that it isn't any of your business, but I'll explain anyway. Lars is my brother. He's excited to be an uncle but worried about his baby sister. I'm lucky he can make time every day to see me, since there are only two doctors in this half of the county."

And doesn't that just put me in my place? Fitz thought wryly.

"Before you ask, Major Nosy-pants, I'm on my own—no husband or boyfriend waiting to meet his son or daughter. No wife or girlfriend either, for that matter." Clara's eyes dared him to question her, but even as her expression challenged him, he could hear a deep hurt in her voice, well-hidden. He recognized it because he was intimately familiar with burying pain.

He wouldn't hurt her by asking. Still, "Major Nosy-pants?" he asked, unable to keep the shocked laughter out of his voice.

"Oh, is it *General* Nosy-pants?" she challenged, and he was glad to hear some of the raw hurt had receded.

"I'm guessing that you don't know much about the Corps, ma'am," he drawled, surprised to find that he wanted to flirt with her. *Was* flirting with her already. Something about this stranger made his heart feel instantly lighter.

"Are you gonna teach me, sailor?" she answered with a saucy tilt to her chin, her response so outrageous he knew she was playing with him.

Before he could answer, he heard someone in the other room. Lars had arrived.

Chapter Three

The man who walked into the room made Fitz glad that he knew Lars was Clara's brother. Fitz was hardly a good judge of masculine beauty, but even he could see the doctor was tall and dark with a face that could have been on an actor in a Hollywood blockbuster romance. The man barely glanced at Fitz before going to Clara's side and hugging her.

"How are you feeling today, Belly? How's the baby's movement? Did you take your blood pressure this morning?"

Clara's expression was so perfectly that of an annoyed baby sister that Fitz had to physically hold in a chuckle that finally escaped as a snort. How the hell could Clara, this near-stranger, make him want to laugh so much when he'd been feeling downright morose even earlier this morning?

"I'm feeling fine, the baby's kicking and my blood pressure was at the high end of normal this morning," she answered, rolling her eyes. "Now, could you please take a look at the *actual* patient?"

Her brother turned as if noticing Fitz for the first time and studied him, his eyes narrowing.

"Ah, yes, the unconscious Marine you found lying in the berry patch who wants to stay away from the hospital," Lars observed dryly. Almost as if he were putting on a doctor costume, his whole attitude changed. He didn't become cold exactly, although Fitz saw a healthy dose of suspicion in the doctor's eyes. It was more that he looked clinical, coolly professional. Fitz felt instantly defensive, but he tried to tamp down the feelings. He owed it to his little angel to try and be nice to her brother who was, after all, also doing him a favor.

"*Retired* Marine," Fitz corrected in a tight voice.

Lars gave a curt nod and moved closer, rolling up his sleeves. "Dr. Lars Olafson," he introduced himself in a clipped tone. "I'd better do a full exam, if you don't mind. I'd much rather you were at least in my clinic or, better still, the hospital, but Clara wouldn't let me come over until I agreed that I wouldn't insist on it."

Fitz darted a questioning glance at Clara. Her face was carefully blank, but he still tried to convey his thanks with his eyes. His good opinion of her was reaffirmed, and maybe even increased, as it was clear she'd meant every word she'd said earlier.

"You can examine me here," he said. He was tempted to refuse, but he wasn't foolish enough not to realize that what Clara had said earlier had been correct. He'd been unconscious for several minutes, for chrissakes, and that meant he'd be stupid to refuse at least some at-home medical care, especially given his recent medical history. He might be a lot of bad things but flat-out stupid wasn't one of them.

"Clara, can you get my bag? I left it in the living room." Lars' tone was offhand, but Clara quirked one auburn eyebrow up skeptically, even as she nodded her agreement.

"*Oh-kay*," she answered, drawing out the syllables. As she walked to door—actually, and he would never use this description out loud, but she looked more like she was waddling than walking—Fitz couldn't believe that he hadn't noticed earlier how oddly she was moving. It was blatantly obvious to him now that she was heavy with child. It just underscored how out of things he must have been when she'd found him.

As soon as Clara had left the room, Lars leaned in very close, and Fitz tensed, ready to defend himself.

"I only have about ten seconds before she comes back so I'll be brief," Lars said in a low, matter-of-fact tone. "I don't know if you are what you seem to be or if you're some sort of criminal. But you've somehow instantly managed to make my sister care about what happens to you. I trust my sister and I love her. I'm not going to report you, but I *will* investigate you, and know this. If you hurt her or the baby in any way, I will never stop searching for you, and when I find you, I *will* make you suffer."

Seamlessly, as if he hadn't said anything, Lars straightened just as Clara returned to the room with his bag, which she set on the bed next to Fitz where Lars had leaned a second earlier. Fitz felt a grudging respect for the man. Lars didn't know exactly who he was dealing with—and Fitz was more dangerous than most career criminals, even without tapping into his family's vast wealth and influence—but the doctor was bravely protective of his sister while also acknowledging that he trusted her. Based on what he'd seen of her so far, Fitz didn't think Clara would appreciate her brother's interference. For himself, he didn't mind it. It almost made him feel more comfortable. Good or bad, this family put it all out there and shot from the hip. He respected that. It even made him feel a twinge of guilt at not having told them exactly who he was.

Clara must have sensed something of the tension in the room because she glanced between them suspiciously, but when neither man reacted, the moment passed.

With a small penlight, Lars examined Fitz's eyes carefully. "Any pain or photosensitivity?" he asked.

"Pain, yeah...one hell of a headache, but nothing intolerable, and definitely no sensitivity to your little mini flashlight there," Fitz answered. Based on the increased concern on her face, he feared his reassuring smile to Clara was more of a grimace.

"That's a good sign, and the headache is...not unexpected," Lars answered. "I'm sorry."

Fitz only had a second to wonder about the surprising apology before the doctor was probing his head. Though Lars' touch was light, it still hurt like hell in one spot. Which, of course, was where he lingered. Fitz wanted to shout, but instead he gritted his teeth and allowed himself one terse grunt as he glared at the doctor.

Finally, after an agonizing moment, Lars straightened and stopped his torture-by-probing. "Your head wound looks okay. It'll need close monitoring, of course, and I'd strongly prefer that you had a CT scan as well." His reproachful stare encompassed Clara as well as Fitz. "However, particularly with your hair so short, I have a good view of the exterior, where the wounds appear to be strictly superficial. And you don't seem to be having any of the red-flag symptoms like confusion, blurred vision, nausea, extreme pallor. Simply put, I'd guess you have an extremely hard head."

A hint of a smile touched Fitz's lips at the unexpectedly blunt comment, and he could see that Clara's eyes sparkled as well. "Is that your professional opinion?" he asked dryly.

The slow torture continued as the doctor probed and flexed his swollen wrist. It was the least of his newest injuries, but it still ached. Then again, Fitz thought it might be easier to count the parts of his body that didn't currently hurt than the ones that did.

"Wrist is definitely sprained, but likely not seriously," Lars observed, and Fitz pulled his arm back to his side.

"All right," Lars continued, "Let's take a look at this knee. I can see the swelling from here, so I think we'll need to cut your pants off, even though I don't like leaving you with nothing to wear."

"My pack should be at the top of the ridge, leaned up against a tree," Fitz offered in his rasping voice, which was close to the way it normally sounded nowadays.

"Good. I can get it before I leave, then," Lars answered.

Fitz was certain that the other man would search it thoroughly, but he wouldn't find anything Fitz minded him knowing. Certainly nothing personal... He didn't carry that sort of thing anymore. "Thanks," he grunted.

"Belly, can you help with the scissors before you leave?" Lars looked at Clara when he spoke, but then turned to Fitz questioningly. "Unless you'd prefer she stay?"

The question felt more significant than just about the exam, and Fitz knew he should say no. He should let her leave the room now, and he should get the hell out of here as fast as he could. It would be smart for him, as messed up as he was, and certainly it would be best for her. But he *liked* her. She made him remember some of the softer things in life that he'd allowed himself to forget — *forced* himself to forget. Like a damned glutton for punishment, he wanted as much of her time as he could have before he had to leave. He looked at her face and the uncertainty there, as if she were afraid she'd offended him, decided him.

"I'd like you to stay," he said, looking at Clara instead of Lars, adding, "if you want to."

She nodded. "Sure."

Clara wasn't sure what had just happened, but something important had passed between her and the stranger. *Fitz.* The intensity and depth in his bright blue eyes convinced her she wasn't imagining it. Somehow, out of nowhere, she thought she might have come across a kindred soul. But then he shuttered his eyes again and she reminded herself that, however kindred he might be, this soldier had been hurt — and not just in body.

Since there were so few doctors in the county, as the daughter of a doctor and now the sister of one, and with her first-aid training, the act of assisting with a patient was very comfortable for her. She took up the scissors without hesitation as Lars held his hands very gently on Fitz's leg. She sliced the fabric cleanly, exposing the swollen knee. It didn't look good, already very puffy and inflamed, and with some dark bruising. That wasn't what made her stifle a gasp, though.

What she'd uncovered of his leg made the scars on his chest look practically neat by comparison. *How did he not lose his leg?* Her heart squeezed in sympathy. *How did he survive the torture of the operations he must have had in order to not lose this leg?* She snuck a sidelong glance at her brother. His professional façade was up and in full force, but she could see that his eyes, so similar to hers in shape and color, had softened. She didn't dare look at Fitz. He seemed proud, and she didn't want to take away from one iota of his dignity with the sympathy she didn't know if she could hide at the moment.

Instead, she set down the scissors and stepped back, letting Lars take her place. She pulled the instant ice-pack out of her brother's bag — their father's gift to him when he'd started medical school — and waited for Lars' instructions. His movements were slow and measured, but Fitz still hissed at one point when Lars turned his knee a bit.

Lars stepped back and frowned. "I really can't tell for sure without an MRI, and with all the edema around the joint — swelling. It could just be bad trauma, or it could be a variety of more serious problems. However...short of seeing the surgeon who performed your previous operation, I think you should treat it with frequent icing and acetaminophen or Motrin as needed. Stay off of it as much as possible, use crutches or a walker if you can."

Fitz snorted at the suggestion, and Lars gave him a quelling look.

"I can do another exam in a week or so." The doctor's expression was coolly professional.

"A week? No." Fitz shook his head and winced at the movement.

"You need to be monitored at least that long for your head injury as well, which it's safest to treat as if it were a moderate concussion," Lars countered.

Clara could feel the tension rising again. She knew her brother and that it had irked him to no end when she'd demanded his promise that he wouldn't take the mysterious stranger to the hospital, no matter what. He would be mad about that for years to come and, boy, could he sulk without appearing to do so, especially at family parties. She'd barely met Fitz, but she'd already seen how determined he was, so she couldn't see him backing down easily on this either.

Like a burst of lightning, so bright it practically made her nerves sizzle, a brilliant idea occurred to her. Fitz was obviously concerned for her welfare, or at least seemed to be from his reaction when she'd told him she was mostly alone in the cabin. She was betting that, while nothing in the world might convince him to do something for his own welfare, he would probably do almost anything if it were someone else's welfare in question—say, *her* welfare and the welfare of her unborn child.

Could she really do it? It wasn't as though it would be a total lie. She *was* eight months pregnant after all. Sure, she knew she'd be okay on her own, as she'd planned to be. Actually, as she'd insisted upon to all her family and friends. But some chores and tasks were getting difficult—like putting on her socks, for instance. Just lately, she was having a lot of trouble sliding the little suckers onto her feet, and soon it was going to be too cold for sandals.

Looking at the firm set of Fitz's chin and the stubborn determination in his eyes where pain still lurked as well, her heart clenched again. She could do it. For some reason, she wanted to do whatever she could for this near-stranger. A little voice whispered that she also just plain wanted to spend more time with him, but she didn't listen to it. She was doing this for his own good. Still, she needed to tread lightly.

"Lars, you should let him leave if he wants to." Both men's heads swiveled toward her in surprise at her words. She put her hands on her hips and tried to look her most defiant. "I mean, you are *ridiculous* with your precautions. Telling me I can't go hiking, or maybe I shouldn't lift a lot of heavy objects around here... Who's going to do that instead? *You*? You're way too busy."

At that outrageous statement, Fitz looked suitably aghast. Lars looked offended for a split second before understanding dawned. It was true that he often urged her to be careful, naturally, but he knew she was exaggerating about hiking, and she always called him to help with anything heavy.

"*Belly*," Lars said in a warning tone, and she wasn't positive if it was part of the act or out of real concern that she not go too far.

"Just last week you were" — she did finger-quotes in the air — "'*seriously concerned*' about those two accidents and that I was having those silly little practice contractions all day and hadn't called you." Clara knew she was laying it on pretty thick, and Lars was hiding a smile, but Fitz just looked more and more disturbed.

"You only knew they were Braxton-Hicks contractions because I, your *doctor*, examined you. For all you knew, they could have been real and you might have delivered at home alone." Lars picked up the fictional thread easily, just as he always had when they'd been kids getting into mischief.

Raising her eyebrow, she went in to clinch it. "I promised to drive into town if I had them badly again, didn't I?" She paused, looking at Fitz surreptitiously from under her eyelashes. He looked deeply troubled. "Anyway, it is everyone's right to make their *own* medical decisions. Even if I would be perfectly happy to have Fitz stay here so I could monitor him, I would *never* insist."

"In good conscience, I can't condone what you're doing alone out here, Clara Belle, nor can I condone Fitz's leaving, but I suppose you're right that you've both left me no choice." Lars' sigh was deep and very put-upon, and Clara resolved to ask him if something was really bothering him. He *had* seemed extremely disturbed by the two accidents she'd had around the house the week before.

"Fitz, there's no way you might have more sense than my little sister and change your mind and take my advice as a physician, is there? Especially knowing that leaving might mean serious injury or harm to you?" Lars prompted, sounding frustrated.

Fitz was quiet for a long moment. The silence in the room stretched so long that Clara had the chance to hear the water of the lake lapping at the dock outside, and rush of the wind through the tall trees that surrounded the cabin. Finally, he answered, "I think maybe I'd better stay after all."

Chapter Four

Once the question of him staying was settled, Lars gave Fitz some medicine and hurried out, telling them he'd need to rush to get the pack from the ridge before he had to begin his morning appointments. Fitz lay back with a heavy sigh and looked suddenly drained, with his eyelids and the corners of his mouth drooping. Clara was frankly amazed at the tenacity he'd shown in staving off the exhaustion for so long. He managed to hide two yawns, but couldn't quite stifle a third, and when she came back into the room after making him a cup of herbal tea, she found him fast asleep and snoring lightly. She paused in the doorway, cradling the warm mug, and marveled at how much more peaceful he looked in repose. The medicine must have helped, because the little lines of strain were gone from his face. She could even make out small creases that showed he was a man who liked to smile or laugh, and who had spent a lot of time in the sun. They only added to his stunning good looks. Still, she decided she'd be sure to offer him sunblock while he was staying with her.

She chuckled to herself at the thought. As if she could make him — this dominant, stubborn ex-soldier — do anything. Then again, she'd *encouraged* him to stay, hadn't she? A pinch of guilt at her own small deception threatened to rise in her chest, but she pushed it right back down again where it belonged. It'd truly been for his own good.

Fitz looked like he'd been running for a long time — hunted, haunted. The last thing he needed was to move again, injured and in pain. Those piercing eyes of his were so sad, so alone — so similar to the eyes she saw looking back at her in her mirror sometimes, though she looked that way less and less often these days. Every cell in her body, every sparkling facet of her soul, urged her to soothe him and help him find some peace. If he didn't, and she knew this from experience that had been hard-won and hope-killingly painful, soon it would become habit. Normal. And it would eat him from the inside out.

She set the cup down on the nightstand, in case he woke up and wanted something warm on his throat. Even after the water, his voice had still sounded rough and grating. From his other injuries? She wouldn't ask, but maybe he'd tell her when he trusted her more. She took the afghan from the foot of the bed — one of very many that her grandmother had knitted over the years — and laid it over him. The air wasn't cold in the cabin, but with one of his pant legs mostly gone, she didn't want him uncomfortable. Satisfied, she slipped out and went back to the living room to start her daily chores.

She quietly washed her breakfast dishes and swept and cleaned the rooms. She thought it must be the famous nesting instinct she'd read about, because she, a lifelong member of the *laissez-faire* school of cleaning and clutter, now couldn't stand a speck of dust in the house. That was one part of pregnancy she wouldn't mind keeping—not to the same degree, but it was kind of nice to have such a tidy little home. She checked on Fitz again afterward, but he hadn't moved even the smallest muscle.

Satisfied, she sat down and opened her laptop to work on some of the remote contract paralegal work that she'd managed to keep when she'd left the Minneapolis law firm where she'd spent several years as a legal assistant and paralegal. The Internet was cooperating for a welcome change, so she managed to get through a few hours of document review of e-mails, memos and countless other miscellaneous documents for mentions of employee pension plans before her stomach warned her it was getting close to lunchtime. In another grand irony of late-pregnancy, she was always *starving* but couldn't eat much at a time. Her brother told her that it was because the baby was taking up so much room that she felt full rapidly. That made sense, but it meant that she constantly fluctuated between being ravenously hungry and painfully full, sometimes at the same time.

And how was her patient? She shut her laptop with a soft snap and stood, with deliberate slowness this time, rubbing her aching lower back. When she looked into the guest bedroom, he lay completely still, but his soft snore still rumbled into the quiet room, and she felt a disproportionate relief. She hated to wake him, but the pain would do that soon enough once the medicine wore off, so he might as well have lunch and more painkillers before he got to that point. Maybe she could ask him to reach something for her. Come to think of it, it *was* harder and harder to get the plates down from the highest shelf. Her belly kept bumping the counter, and she couldn't seem to stretch as far as she'd used to.

Frankly, Lars hadn't been the only one rattled by the recent accidents, either. First, she must have left the watering can out in the middle of the path to the outhouse, which was ridiculous since, of all places, that was one where she had to go with increasing frequency at all hours of the day and night. Oddly, though, she had no recollection of moving the can that day. She hadn't even watered anything with it that recently, since there had been a decent amount of natural rainfall. Still, she'd nearly tripped and fallen right over it on her way to the bathroom one evening, and she thanked goodness that she still had some of her formerly quick reflexes to do a deft side-step and brace herself on a tree. She wondered if maybe a bear had somehow moved it, but that wasn't a terribly comforting alternative to her own temporary insanity.

The second accident had been more disturbing, though. She'd been down at the dock, using the ladder to hold on to while she reached one toe down into the chilly water and the whole thing, ladder, rails and bolts, had just come right off and sent her plunging into the water, fully-clothed. Luckily, she was a strong swimmer and hadn't bumped anything on the way down, so she'd just been able to swim in to shore — but it could have been serious. The weirdest thing was that the ladder was only a year old, and it had felt rock-steady when she and her best friend had used it a couple of weeks earlier. Clara wasn't unhappy to have someone else around the cabin, however temporarily, if only to save her from her own dumb mistakes.

She began heating some tomato soup over one gas ring and was in the process of grilling a few cheese sandwiches in a pan on the other when she heard a groan and half of a curse from the other room, quickly silenced. She curved her lips up in amusement that she couldn't stifle, but she tamped it down when she heard the telltale creaking of the floor that meant her patient was on the move. She turned and prepared to chide Fitz for putting pressure on his knee so soon, but when she saw him, the scolding died on her lips. With his hair mussed, his face much more rested and the ridiculous sight of his mismatched pant legs, one normal and the other cut high on his thigh, she couldn't bring herself to be too angry.

"You shouldn't be on that knee," she admonished without heat.

He had the good grace to look a little sheepish. "I know. I just…can't stand being in bed when I'm awake."

"Oh, really?" She quirked an eyebrow speculatively. "You must be very…*creative* with your girlfriends, then." Some imp of mischief, almost beyond her control, had prompted her words, but she didn't want to take them back. It felt so good to flirt again, to feel like a woman. Which was kind of silly, since she was hugely pregnant and talking to a near-stranger, but there it was.

Her comment surprised a bark of laughter from him, and he studied her consideringly. Appreciatively. "No girlfriends. I, ah…" He trailed off and she could have sworn she saw a guilty flush on his cheeks. What was he thinking about? "You are what my grandfather would call '*a real corker*'."

Clara narrowed her eyes. "Is that a good thing?"

Fitz grinned, the smile spreading slowly until it was wide across his face, showing rows of gleaming, white teeth and dimple in his cheek. Clara had to suck in a quick breath at how gorgeous and charming it made him.

"It is an excellent thing, Clara Belle," he answered, his eyes curiously intent, even while they sparkled.

The acrid smell of something burning recalled Clara to the sandwiches, which were now starting to blacken on one side.

"Oh, shoot!" she exclaimed, switching off the gas and waving one hand over the pan to dissipate the smoke, which had started to rise. "I'll make some more, I'm sorry," she apologized.

"I've had worse. I don't mind. It's my fault for distracting you, after all."

Clara's heart thudded painfully, and her skin went hot with awareness at Fitz's rasping voice so close behind her. He must have crossed the room without her noticing, distracted as she was by the burning food. He sure could move quickly in spite of his injuries and scars.

"No...I couldn't serve you burnt grilled cheese." She felt flustered and flushed, warm with embarrassment and awareness.

"Nah, I mean it. Don't worry. It'll put hair on my chest."

Clara's head came up with a snap, and her eyes felt suspiciously misty. "I haven't heard anyone say that since my dad passed away."

Fitz's smile was gentle, and a look of understanding passed between them. "One of my grandfather's favorite sayings. My grandmother wasn't much of a cook. That's why..." Fitz broke off and looked awkward.

Clara took pity on him. "It was a very nice thing for him to say, then. It sounds as if I might like your grandfather." She regretted the last part of her comment, realizing that it was more likely that Fitz's grandfather was deceased than that he was still alive. She still mourned the recent passing of her own grandfather, and grief could come at the most unexpected times.

Fitz answered the question that she hadn't asked. "I think he'd really enjoy meeting you, too. He has good days and bad days...but still more good than bad. He's too stubborn by half, though." Something that could have been regret passed over his expression, quickly hidden.

"Ah, so you come by it naturally," Clara quipped, and she liked how her comment changed his eyes from cold and carefully expressionless to amused again.

"Yes, stubborn-as-a-pack-mule definitely runs in my family." And just like that, his expression was dark and closed again. Clara realized that she still held the pan out, and she could hear the soup bubbling away in the background.

"You *can't* seriously want one of these," she said, motioning at the charred bread.

Before she could stop him, Fitz reached out and wrenched one from the pan, only getting half of it while the rest remained stuck in a mass of blackened, gooey cheese. He popped it into his mouth and crunched determinedly.

Even though the sandwich must still be practically molten, and she could hear how crisply burned it was from the sound of his chewing, he choked down one large piece with every sign of enjoyment. A few crumbs formed a black, dusty mustache on his upper lip.

"Delicious," he pronounced, and put the remainder of the half he'd managed to pry off the pan into his mouth. Something thawed then melted in the region of her heart when he swallowed that, too, and reached for the rest. It stuck there stubbornly, glued to the pan, in spite of Fitz's valiant efforts.

Their eyes met, and his were determined and kind as he tried to work the piece free to no avail.

"I, ah, think I need a spatula," he finally admitted.

Like a wave rising up and breaking on the shore, amusement filled her from her toes to her chest, finally spilling out as a peal of laughter, continuing into a wheezing laugh. Fitz laughed as well, the sound rusty as though he were out of practice.

"They're *horrible*," she gasped between laughs. "Admit it. They're like charcoal."

"I will *never* say that," he answered diplomatically, setting her laughter off harder.

"Okay, you don't have to say it," she panted out. "But that doesn't mean it isn't true. Now, I'm going to put the remains of these truly sad sandwiches out of their misery and set this pan to soak. We'll eat something else."

When she went to scrape the charred remains off the pan into the trash can, the hard, callused surface of Fitz's hand over hers stopped her. She looked up at him inquiringly.

"I will be grateful to eat *anything* you cook for me. I appreciate it." His voice was low and earnest, and she felt tears threatening again. *Stupid hormones can't even handle a handsome man being nice to me.*

"Thank you," she mumbled in a husky voice. "Now *please* let me make something better?"

"Agreed under protest," he replied, but she could hear the smile in his voice. "Let me take care of the pan, at least." He took it from her hands, his rough fingers sliding against her soft palm and sending sparks of awareness throughout her body again. She let him take the offending cookware and turned back to the counter quickly to cover her reaction. The poor man was just being nice, for heaven's sake. *Isn't he?*

The soup was miraculously unburned, and she put together chicken salad sandwiches with some of the leftover roast chicken that Lars had brought her the day before, along with mayonnaise, tomatoes, onions and cheddar cheese.

She studied Fitz as he eased himself onto one of her grandmother's spindly kitchen chairs. He grimaced, but considering the extent of his injuries, he was doing surprisingly well. Stubbornness obviously had its benefits.

"I only have milk, water or seltzer," she apologized as she put a chipped plate down in front of him. "Oh, or tea," she added.

"That's fine, Clara. Anything you give me to drink will be wonderful." His tone was so honest, in his deep and rumbling voice, that she believed him. It warmed her from the inside out and took away her embarrassment.

She poured him some seltzer in a glass.

"No bendy straw?" he asked, and she snorted.

"I think you can drink like a big boy now, hm?" Again, she liked the rush of flirting with him.

"Yes, I'm a very big boy. A big man, in fact. Thank you for noticing," he returned, and lifted the glass to his lips. Her mouth went dry as she watched the strong column of his neck work as he swallowed, his eyes never leaving her face.

A firm kick to her midsection from the inside reminded her that someone else was waiting for lunch, too, and her lips curved up in a smile as she rubbed her belly. "One minute, little one," she said, then darted at a glance at Fitz when she realized how weird it might seem that she had gotten into the habit of talking to the baby almost continuously since she'd moved out here alone. But he wasn't looking at her face. His expression was one of total and complete awe as his gaze remained at stomach height.

"*Holy*— I *saw* that! I saw your stomach move from here, like an alien trying to escape!"

Clara knew she ought to be offended, and she tried to work up a good mad, but all she felt was mirth at his ill-chosen but very honest words. She chuckled.

"While his or her father could aptly be described as a snake, weasel or cockroach, he is, in fact, fully human," she answered wryly.

Fitz's expression was thoroughly abashed as if just realizing what he'd said. "I am...*so sorry*. Again. And sorry I'm continually apologizing to you."

Clara waved his apology away. "I'm not really offended. I had almost the same thought the first time I got a really hard kick. It's bizarre and incredible at the same time, isn't it? To think that I have another, tiny human living inside of me blows my mind. Let's eat before this little baby gets even feistier though, eh?"

They ate in silence for a while as Clara was too intent on getting as much food into her mouth and stomach as quickly as possible to speak. When she'd finished her sandwich, she saw that Fitz must have been nearly as hungry as she was. Only crumbs remained on his plate, and he was eyeing them as if he might lick them right off, too.

"Good?" she asked.

"Thoroughly delicious. I can't think when I've enjoyed a sandwich and soup more," he answered. "Thank you for cooking, ma'am. It's been a long time since someone made a home-cooked meal for me."

Torn between chiding him for calling her 'ma'am' again, and being intrigued by how sad his voice had sounded at the end, Clara held her tongue. She would bide her time so she wouldn't scare him off right away.

"I'm glad you liked it, but a sandwich and a can of soup isn't really cooking." She laughed.

Fitz looked away. "It is where I come from."

It made some sense. In the military they probably had rations and communal meals, not home cooking, although he was out of the service now.

"How long were you in the Marines?" she asked, kicking herself instantly for breaking her own decision to stay silent and not pry just now.

"Twelve years." He surprised her by answering. "Well, twelve and a half, I suppose, but I don't count the last six months, since they were all in hospitals." His expression was funny, as if he'd surprised himself by saying so much, then went shuttered again in the way she was already coming to recognize.

How awful it must have been for this active, vital man to spend six months in hospitals—in pain, restricted. No wonder he wanted to avoid them. Clara practically itched to know more, but his face stopped her. That was enough for now.

"How's the pain in your knee now?" she asked, changing the subject.

Fitz grunted noncommittally, which she took to mean that he was in pain but didn't want to say it. Well, it was no surprise. She rose heavily, belly-first, and went to the cupboard where she kept a supply of acetaminophen and took out two more pills.

"It's time for some more of these."

For a moment, it looked as if Fitz would refuse the little white pills she held out in her hand, but good sense obviously prevailed and he took them, washing them down with the last of his seltzer.

"More seltzer? Or anything else?" She motioned toward the fridge.

Fitz shook his head and grimaced. His head must be hurting again as well.

"Thanks, but I'm stuffed to the gills with your delicious food, Ms. Olafson."

Clara laughed at his overly formal tone. "And my not-so-delicious food, too, which I hope doesn't give you indigestion, Mr...." She trailed off. "I know my brother introduced himself, so you know our last name, but I don't know *your* last name." Well, there went more of her restraint. She wished she could recall the question, but Fitz surprised her again by answering.

"Retired Master Sergeant Colin Fitzhugh, ma'am, at your service."

"Fitzhugh, huh?" She laughed. "That's a pretty famous name around these parts."

Fitz didn't say anything, and no spark of recognition lit his expression.

"You must not be from around here." Clara laughed again. "Fitzhugh Manufacturing is one of the top three employers in the Twin Cities and all of Minnesota. The Fitzhugh family is like Minnesota's version of the Kennedys. Everyone wants to know them." She tried to keep the bitterness out of her voice but didn't quite succeed.

"I take it you're not a fan?" Fitz asked.

Clara pursed her lips, seeing Brock's face all over again in her mind's eye. The face she'd once found so handsome and charming, but which she now realized had hidden a shallow, greedy little soul and complete lack of substance. She could hear his voice in her head when she'd gone over to his apartment, nervous but generally more excited than anything else to share the news that they would be parents. *"What? Did you honestly think I would* marry *you? Why would I ever tie myself to a little nobody glorified secretary when I go to parties with people like the* Fitzhughs? *You're just a distraction, and you're not even the only one. You miscalculated on this one, Miss Olafson. Big time."*

Shaking off the memory, which still had the power to stab her like a knife to the chest—more at how stupid she'd been not to see Brock's true nature sooner than anything else at this point—she recalled herself to the present.

"To be fair, I don't know any of them personally, nor would I ever seek to. I don't even know that much about them. I just know some of the company that they keep, and if you can measure someone by their friends…" She let the sentence hang. What did it matter what she thought of the illustrious Fitzhughs? Her Fitz obviously wasn't one of them and didn't know anything about them. She smiled and shook her head. "Why the heck am I rambling on about the dang Fitzhughs when you must be dying to stretch your leg out and put your head back down on something soft?"

"I'm fine," he grunted, but the little lines that had reappeared around his mouth betrayed his lie.

"I'm sure you are, Sergeant Surly, but maybe I'm nicely trying to tell you that I need some peace and quiet to finish my work." Clara softened her words with another winning smile. As she'd hoped, making it about her convenience as opposed to his own comfort seemed to convince Fitz at least partially.

Reluctance was in every line of his body as he stood, though, along with stiffness.

"Go on, *shoo!*" She waved her hands as she spoke laughingly. "I don't want to see you until suppertime, all right?"

Fitz held up his hands in a gesture of surrender, but his eyes told her that she wasn't fooling him entirely. "All right, all right. Whatever you say, *ma'am.*" He drawled the last word so that it sounded almost like an endearment before he moved and winced.

Clara jutted her chin out and tried to look stern.

With one last sidelong look, he shuffled heavily back to the guest room, and she only relaxed when she heard the telltale creaking of the bedframe. He was going to be a difficult patient. Still, she somehow felt more alive than she had in months, more like herself. Hopeful not only for her child — she had always been thrilled about the baby — but for herself too. And she had a gruff, guarded, sinfully handsome retired soldier to thank for that.

His leg, head and even his wrist were starting to throb like hell again by the time he got settled back into the old brass bed, but Fitz took the pain in stride. He couldn't believe how close he'd come to slipping up and telling Clara things that he never told anyone. *No one.* His fall must have affected more than his body and scrambled his ever-loving brain, too. First, he'd almost told her that his grandmother was such a horrible cook that his grandfather had hired a full-time chef. Marcel was a wonderful chef, a terrible liar, a proud French-Canadian and like an uncle to Fitz, but it was pretty unusual to have a private chef living with your family. Then he'd gone and told her his full name. *Holy hell.* He was lucky that she didn't follow his family, or she'd know just who he was. Even after all this time, he still got the occasional mention in the society pages, to his consternation.

He supposed that at least now he knew where he stood. She disliked his family by reputation. *Fair enough.* He wasn't too crazy about them in general, either. His father had been an utter ass, and his mother had become a mean, bitter woman intent on making everyone feel inferior to her. Even his oldest brother, Drew, now the head of Fitzhugh Manufacturing and pretty much the head of the family as well, since their grandfather's health had declined, was a self-righteous prick most of the time. They hadn't spoken in several years and hadn't seen each other in much longer. He couldn't imagine the wholesome Clara approving of some of his family's choices, and she didn't seem likely to have her head turned by wealth and status. He supposed it was good to know the lay of the land so he could avoid missteps.

For some reason, he really wanted her to like *him*. To respect *him...Fitz.* It was more important to him than he could have imagined after such a short time. He could tell her who he really was once she'd gotten to know him. And if a little voice niggled at the back of his head, reminding him that dishonesty by omission was still dishonesty? Well, too damn bad. Only a very few of his closest friends in the Corps knew of his true lineage, and he liked to keep it that way.

When he'd been younger, he'd unashamedly used the power and influence gifted to him by his name and nothing else to get whatever he'd wanted, whenever and however. But since he'd joined the Marine Corps, he'd grown to love the anonymity of being judged for himself, not for who his family was. He only told people when he was sure that their opinion of him wouldn't change, and that moment never came for some people. *Truth be told, for a lot of people.*

Outside of Minnesota, Wisconsin, Iowa and the Dakotas — and maybe Chicago — being a Fitzhugh really didn't have much of a cachet, anyway. However, especially in Minnesota, his family had some sort of special, hallowed status that made a lot of people go googly-eyed when they found out his name. He didn't even like coming back to the Upper-Midwest for that reason, and he normally didn't, except for brief visits with his grandfather, but he'd had to come for Abe — for Abe's family — to tell them he was sorry, so *damn* sorry.

He closed his mind against the memories that threatened to choke him, of the blood, death and destruction, all baking under a hot desert sky so blue that no clouds ever came to cool it. Still, a few memories crept in — the smell of flesh burning, his own flesh burning from the IED they'd driven over, Abe's young face, twisted with agony as Fitz promised him — *promised* him — that he'd make it. Then the peace in Abe's expression when his spirit had finally left his body, too badly burned and injured inside, they'd later told him, to have ever had a chance.

Fitz's cheeks felt cool, and he swiped at them angrily when he realized a few tears had leaked out of his eyes. *No.* He was damn well not doing this now, not thinking about the guilt that ate at him day and night, making his sleep restless and his days long. *So goddamn long.*

Instead, he turned his thoughts to the pretty little frizzy-haired Clara with her gentle touch and sassy wit, sparkling hazel eyes that watched him with what might be more than friendly compassion. Her image was like the cool rain that never fell on the parched land of his nightmares, and it soothed his thoughts. In spite of the pain, even more intense than usual and layered on top of the never-ending aches that radiated from his twisted and mangled left side, he slept.

Chapter Five

Fitz was having 'the dream' again. It was part of why he hated sleeping so much, because at night his memories could creep around the defenses he kept so firmly in place during the day and force him back to everything he never wanted to see again. Dry heat, pain, fire...but this time, when he looked down at Abe, it was his little rescuer's face he saw instead — Clara he held in his arms. Her face was pale, and she looked ill, a sheen of sweat coating her waxy skin.

"You promised me...just like you promised Abe. I trusted you to keep me safe," *she whispered in a voice thick with tears. Fitz tried desperately to hold the spark of her life to him, but he could practically feel her slipping away.*

When he surged upright at the soft touch of the real Clara's hand on his arm, the quick movement made every muscle in his body burn. It took a second for her face — her pink-cheeked, vibrant, *living* face — to come into focus. The relief he felt nearly dropped the bottom right out of his stomach.

"*Thank God,*" he whispered, reaching out before he could stop himself and tracing the warm, downy velvet of her cheek with his fingertips. She stood still, watching him with an odd mixture of compassion and surprised interest—or maybe he flattered himself about the interest. When he realized what he was doing, he snatched his hand back.

She shook her head. "It's okay. I'm sorry I woke you." She bit her lip and looked down. "I wouldn't have but you, ah, seemed to be having a *really* bad dream."

He grunted, gingerly swinging his legs to the side of the bed and testing the feel of pressure on his knee. It still hurt like a son of a bitch, but it was significantly better than it had been the day before. The pain in his head had decreased to a dull throb, too.

"It could be dangerous to wake me up like that, Clara. The things I have in my past…some of them are pretty ugly. Violent." His throat was dry, and his words sounded raspy as he warned her in a low voice.

She should have stepped back—that tone designed to make grown men give him a wide berth—but instead she took a step closer to him, the air around her carrying the faint scent of some sort of fruity shampoo mixed with what he could have sworn was sunshine.

"You would never hurt me. I can tell."

He wished he felt the same confidence he heard in her voice. "I would never *mean* to hurt you, but it doesn't mean I wouldn't…*won't.*" He scrubbed his hand down his face, the scratchy stubble that had grown over the past day rough against his palm. "I shouldn't have stayed here. I wanted to help, but it could be dangerous for you."

The soft weight of her hand as she touched his shoulder and the heat radiating from her, warmed more than his skin.

"Do you want to talk about whatever it is that you were looking for alone in the deep woods at dawn on a Tuesday?" Her question was soft, tempting him to answer in a way that none of the mandatory therapy sessions he'd attended had ever tempted him.

He wished it were that easy. "Do *you* want to talk about why you would choose to stay out here alone with no running water and a baby coming any day?" he countered.

Her answering smile was wry. "Can we call a truce, then? Or make a mutual non-aggression pact? Isn't that a term you military guys like to use?"

"That sounds like Washington claptrap, ma'am, but I understand the notion." He twitched his lips with the beginning of a reluctant smile.

"Let's shake on it, then, Ensign Enigma," she answered, thrusting one hand toward him.

His stifled laugh came out as a snort, and now he was certain that he hadn't laughed this much in years. But she was ridiculous, such sweetness and light wrapped up in a gorgeous, curvy little package.

"Yes, ma'am," he drawled in response. He meant for the handshake to be brief, just a perfunctory up-and-down motion, but when his skin met the silk of hers, he felt a jolt of awareness that had him shifting uncomfortably and worrying that she could see more than he'd like through the thin pajama bottoms he'd put on from the pack Lars had brought him.

"You going to keep that?" Clara teased, and he realized he'd been holding on to her hand, enjoying the feel of it, for way too long. He released her fingers as if he'd been burned, then felt silly...until he saw how rosy her cheeks had grown. Her eyes looked more green than brown today, and the morning sun made them practically glow. It made him feel marginally better that he hadn't imagined her awareness...wasn't the only one affected by their touch.

"I'm, um, going to make breakfast...lots of breakfast. A heap of steaming, delicious breakfast for a big, delicious man like you—" She broke off with a gasp and covered her mouth with her hand as if belatedly trying to stifle the words she'd already spoken. "I mean, a hunk...a *chunk*! A chunk of *bacon* and a mess of eggs and a fluffy mountain of pancakes... That's what you need. That's what I meant to say...*all* I meant to say."

He didn't know how he held in the laughter this time, but she looked so embarrassed that he took pity on her and nodded as if she'd made perfect sense.

"Of course...naturally, that's what you meant. But, Clara, there's no need to make a fuss. I told you I'd love anything you did for me...uh, *cooked* for me." Was she contagious? Now he was doing it too.

She beamed back at him and suddenly he would have been willing to tumble down the steep slope again, just to see the way that smile lit up her whole face.

"All right, then," she answered, and with a rustle of fabric from the old-fashioned apron she wore, she was gone.

* * * *

To Clara, it seemed like their mutual attraction combined with evasiveness that morning set the rhythm for their interactions over the next few days. The cabin was small, so they were practically on top of each other most of the time, but by silent consent, they stayed away from one another as much as possible, except at mealtimes. The second night, Clara cooked a simple meal of spaghetti and meatballs with garlic bread, which Fitz pronounced the most delicious pasta he'd ever eaten. He flirted a little more, too, and she enjoyed their light conversation, but it was clear that any deeper subject matter was still off the table. She also discovered that the man loved ice cream even more than her cooking, so she made sure to serve it to him for dessert at lunch and dinner every day. She'd genuinely thought her supply of ice cream had been expansive, given her status as a woman in late-pregnancy with heartburn that could singe the fur off a cat at fifty paces, but it began to dwindle dangerously.

Fitz remained close-lipped about his past—and his future—which was fine with her for the moment. She didn't want to talk much about herself either, although she did clarify, much to Fitz's amusement, that Lars hadn't, in fact, given her the nickname 'Belly' due to her pregnancy. Instead, she'd had to live with it much, much longer, though he did seem to take a particular brotherly glee in using it now. Fitz moved around more and more, which Lars had said wasn't the smartest idea but was acceptable with *"extreme caution"*. Lars certainly hadn't cleared him for chopping wood or carrying buckets of water, but Fitz took on those chores and more—peppered with a lot of breaks, at least. He'd obviously watched her, noticing what tasks were becoming almost impossible.

Even though they stayed away from danger-zone topics, Clara enjoyed their conversations. She realized that she liked Fitz — *really* liked him. He felt like an old friend, someone she could trust. And he fit perfectly into the little cabin. She looked forward to seeing him in the morning and to sharing meals with him. It gave her pleasure to cook for him — to see the slow smile on his face as he tasted something she'd made, and to hear his over-the-top compliments on the food, delivered with a grin that showed his dimple.

She snuck peeks at him outside throughout the day through the white, cotton curtains on the windows. Even as he recovered from his injuries, it was a joy to watch his strong, well-made body, in spite of his pain, or maybe it was *because* he worked through the hurt. His eyes betrayed the demons that clearly still dogged him, but physically he refused to give in. He just paused, regrouped, gritted his teeth and continued. Sometimes she thought she surprised him looking at her, too, when he thought she wasn't paying attention. Every time that happened, it made her heart thump and her cheeks grow hot, though she did her best to ignore the growing attraction.

On the fourth day of Fitz's stay, listening to the soothing rhythm of the clunk, clunk, clunk as, sitting on a short stool, he chopped wood in the clearing behind the cabin, she finished the last of the contract work that she'd had. She e-mailed what would be her final summary of the last thousand documents she'd reviewed to Mr. Lacey, of Carter, Lacey & Shaw LLP, the firm that she supposed was now really her former employer. She e-mailed Connie then, too. The older office manager had always been a dear friend to her in her years at the firm, and even though she'd never liked Brock, the other woman had never judged Clara for what had happened, during her relationship with the young junior partner and afterward—unlike so many others.

Dear Connie, she typed. *Attached please find the summary of the last of the documents, and where appropriate, they have been annotated in the DMS. I sent the summary to Mr. Lacey directly as well, under separate cover. As discussed, this means that my remote access can now be disabled. You or Mr. Lacey can call my cell phone, or my brother Lars' satellite phone if there are any questions, moving forward.* She paused, hesitating over the keys. *Thank you again, and I truly appreciate everything. Best, Clara.*

After she'd hit *Send*, she sat there for a long moment, feeling curiously numb.

That was the end, then, of her years as first a filing clerk, then a paralegal and finally a senior paralegal and office assistant, particularly to Mr. Lacey, at one of the preeminent corporate defense law firms in the Twin Cities. She looked down at her outfit—yoga pants with a super-stretchy waist band and a cotton maternity top, all covered by a wooly button-down sweater to ward off the increasing chill that crept into the morning air more and more each day. She could only button the top two buttons now. She wore slippers, and her feet and ankles were swollen like two mini hams. Worse, they were cold, but she hadn't had a prayer of getting her socks on her feet this morning and she couldn't bring herself to ask Fitz to help.

At that thought—the final indignity—her eyes stung and filled with hot tears that spilled out and rolled down her face. She struggled to catch her breath as they threatened to choke her, and her frame shook with the effort.

A noise made her look up toward the door, and she saw Fitz hurrying as much as he could with his limping gait. His eyes were no longer guarded, as they had mostly been over the past few days. Instead, they were a clear, beautiful azure, blazing with concern—maybe even tenderness. He moved her laptop to the side with a care that was surprising, given how worried he looked. He sat down on her scarred coffee table, taking her hands into his.

"What's wrong, honey? I could hear you crying from outside."

The endearment, and the way he looked at her and held her hands, as if she were the most precious thing in the world, made her sob harder. She shook her head and sniffed inelegantly.

"Is it the baby? Should I call your brother?" he asked, starting to rise to get the phone.

"No...*no*," she managed, shaking her head again and feeling ashamed but totally unable to calm her breathing down enough to stop crying.

Fitz sat back down and looked incongruously helpless. He was a little sweaty from his work, with a dark V of perspiration at the throat of his T-shirt, and woodchips clung to his short hair. Every line of his body was strong and masculine, but the emotion in his eyes was soft—almost bewildered in the face of her outburst.

"Finished...work," she gasped, and he inclined his chin.

"Okay, baby, that sounds like a good thing," he answered cautiously.

She nodded back. "Yes, but...that's *it*. That's *all* the work. And now I'm..." she choked on the words but pressed on. "Unemployed, single, pregnant...and my feet are *cold*."

It was muddled, but miraculously, Fitz seemed to understand. He shifted to the couch so that he sat next to her and scooped her up right onto his lap before she knew what was happening.

"I'm too heavy!" she protested in a watery voice.

"*Never*." His answer was low and emphatic, and it made goosebumps rise on her arms. His warm, spicy scent enveloped her as his huge arms surrounded her, holding her close. Her head fit so perfectly in the spot just between his neck and shoulder that it was as if it had always been destined to rest there. He held her quietly, stroking her back, for long moments until she calmed.

It felt wonderful, being held by him, and Clara realized it had been a long time since she'd felt this close to anyone — or maybe she never had. Fitz, with his shadowed eyes and wounded body, understood her in a way she wasn't sure she even understood herself most of the time.

"I'm so sorry," she mumbled against his throat, too embarrassed by her emotional explosion to look at him.

"Don't be, honey." His reply rumbled through his chest against her side, and the vibrations were soothing but also sparked a deeper awareness inside her. She thought she might never get tired of hearing his deep, rasping voice.

"It's hard to leave something behind. Did you work there long?" His tone was gentle, but not patronizing.

She gave a dry laugh that held a hint of bitterness. "Six years — pretty much all of my adult career."

"And they didn't want to keep you on? Because of the pregnancy?" he guessed.

"No," she started carefully. "It's...complicated. I don't really want to work there, either. It's just...so much of who I thought I was. I worked hard, the first one there and the last to leave when things heated up for big cases or clients. People trusted me, and I trusted them. They nicknamed me 'Clarity', for goodness' sake. I wore suits and high heels and I felt like I was important." Clara lifted her head to look at him as she spoke, and the sympathy and understanding—real comprehension—she saw in his eyes almost made her start crying again.

"Were you happy?"

His question gave her pause, and she had to really think about it before she answered. "Maybe once, but no...not anymore. Certainly not since...well, not for a while."

"Ah, so maybe this was the end of a dream, and you're mourning it. A path that you chose that didn't take you where you wanted."

Clara was stunned by how totally he'd nailed her emotions down with one sentence. "Yes, that's exactly it."

"It's healthy to grieve for something you thought you wanted, to get it out of the way and make room for the future—for you and your baby and all the good stuff ahead of you." His words hung in the silent cabin, so simple yet so profound.

What he said made perfect sense, and Clara realized with surprise that she totally agreed. She quirked an eyebrow. "That's great advice, Sergeant. Have you ever thought about taking it, too?"

Now it was Fitz's turn to look away. He was so quiet that she barely even heard his breathing. Her grandmother's old wind-up clock ticked gently from the wall. When he turned back, his eyes still held the grief she'd become accustomed to, but they also held determination. "Maybe I will do just that, Clara Belle."

He shifted again and changed the subject with his movement. "Now, what's this about cold feet?"

"It's nothing, really," she answered, shifting in embarrassment at having confessed that earlier. Practically shouted it in his face, actually. Honesty prompted her to add, "I just...can't get my socks on at all now."

Fitz surprised her by chuckling. "What a pair we are. I'm too stubborn to take my own damn advice and you're too proud to tell me you need help." He rubbed her leg absently as he spoke, leaving sparkling awareness in the wake of his touch. "Will you let me help you with your socks, honey?"

Again, when he caught her gaze, she sensed that he was asking about more than just socks. Something bigger was at play, and while she wasn't sure if she was comfortable, and she was darn sure she wasn't ready, she couldn't help but nod her agreement.

His touch moved lower down her leg until the warm hardness of his hand reached one of her ankles where he began rubbing in a gentle circle. "You do feel cold," he said against her hair.

She had to stop herself from groaning with pleasure at how warm and soothing his touch felt, and she couldn't quite stop the sound when he took her other foot into his other hand.

The look he gave her was surprised at first, then grew warmer. His eyes gleamed. "Good?"

"*Unbelievable*," she whispered in reply, not trusting herself to speak any louder. She let her head fall back against his shoulder, closing her eyes in pleasure.

"You're so damn real, Clara. It's gorgeous," he growled, and it was the only warning she had before he covered her mouth with his.

The warm, faintly minty taste of him was wonderful. Addictive. And the feel of his soft lips moving against hers was like heaven, making all her nerves fire at once. She opened her mouth to allow him more access, and he groaned as he deepened the kiss. He was tentative at first, as if waiting for her permission. She moaned with pure bliss as he swept his tongue against hers, tugging and nibbling at her lips. He surrounded her with his muscular arms and crushed her to him, making her feel delicate and powerful all at once. It had been *so long* since she'd felt this sensual awareness — this dark and urgent need — that she was practically overcome by it. She wasn't sure she'd ever felt it, certainly not with Brock.

She stiffened slightly as that thought of her ex-boyfriend crept into her mind. *Jeez*, even thoughts of him were kind of insidious. She didn't think Fitz would notice, but she should have realized he'd pick up on it since he seemed able to read her like an open book. He stilled and pulled back. When she dared a look up at him, regret was in every line of his roughly handsome features. Even though she still sat on his lap, nestled in his arms, it was as if a thick wall had gone up between them…again.

"Please don't do that," she blurted out before she could stop herself.

As he was so adept at doing, he'd made his face blank again…impassive. But the flicker in his eyes revealed his surprise. She was coming to recognize his tell — very subtle, but unmistakable in the depths of his expressive eyes.

"I shouldn't have kissed you...touched you that way." Low and urgent, the words sounded wrung from him.

"Did you hear me complaining?"

The ghost of a smile touched the corners of his mouth, but his mouth hardened again when guilt crept back into his face. "Of course not, but it doesn't matter. You're vulnerable and I...I'm screwed up, Clara. There's nothing about me that's good enough for someone like you."

"Someone like me?" she asked, torn between being annoyed and flattered.

Fitz's face softened again when he answered. "Beautiful. Sassy and funny, smart as all hell, sad but still soft and kind underneath it."

The warmth that had cooled so abruptly when he'd broken off their kiss melted something in her chest all over again at his words. His voice had gotten a little less scratchy over the past few days, but it was still rough and rumbling. It made everything he said sound raw and honest.

"Thank you," she replied, a depth of emotion behind the words. It meant a lot to hear such sweet words from him, though the context left a bit to be desired. "But what do you think you are that's so different?" she prompted.

"I'm a formerly selfish ass who turned his life around in the Corps, but I miscalculated on my last mission...badly. It cost my division heavily. Really severe injuries and one...casualty." His voice cracked a little on the word. "Part of me is pieced back together, but the rest of me is still...splintered. I'm not a partner, maybe not even a good man. I'm not sure."

Clara heard the anguish as well as the resolve behind his words. It was the most he'd said about himself, and it made her chest and throat tighten with sadness for him, how much he had gone through, how much guilt he carried. She wanted to wrap her arms around him and make him understand that he was a good man. She could see it, plain as day. But she sensed that he'd decided he wasn't, and she didn't know if she could change his mind. She'd been hurt so badly when she'd misjudged a man before. How much more would it hurt this time if she threw her whole being into convincing Fitz and he still decided to walk away, whatever his reasons? She needed time to think — to really consider. Maybe they both needed some space.

"I can't say that I agree, but I do respect you, Fitz." She moved awkwardly off his lap, blushing as her movements made her press up against the hard planes of his muscles again before she stood next to him. "If it's what you want, I'm willing to pretend this" — she gestured between the two of them — "didn't happen."

The blue depths of Fitz's eyes were almost unfathomable, incredibly sad and filled with regret one instant but grimly determined the next. Resolved. "I appreciate that, honey. I think it's best. And it won't happen again."

Clara's heart sank at his words. "You'll still stay, though? Until you're recovered?" She tried to keep the emotion out of her voice.

Fitz's expression softened and his eyes were curiously intent as they watched her. Like two white-hot flames. "I'll stay as long as you need me, Clara."

She nodded jerkily, her eyes suddenly stinging again at the tenderness she heard in his promise. She supposed she should be grateful, and she was...but she wished so much he was promising something else—which was silly.

"I'm going to get a breath of fresh air," she mumbled. She mentally kicked herself at how inane that must sound, but she needed to escape for a moment. She practically fled outside and down to the dock by the lake, cold feet and ankles be darned.

Fitz heard the screen door slam behind her before he'd even registered what she'd said. He'd been so focused on the thickness in her voice—the thickness that sounded like tears. *Damn and double damn me for putting them there.* The last thing he'd wanted to do was hurt her when all she'd been was kind and generous. He'd just wanted to comfort her. But when, as he held the warm, soft curves of her body in his arms and on his lap, she'd looked up at him with her beautiful hazel eyes, her pink lips a little pursed as she'd made that sexy little moan of pleasure at his touch, his control had just snapped. He'd *needed* to touch her, to be closer to her. And damn, that kiss had been amazing. Every other kiss from his misspent youth and even from the rare flings he'd had while he had been in the Corps—they all faded into the background, into oblivion, in the face of the feel of Clara's lips against his. She'd tasted a little like herbal tea with a trace of salt from her tears, but oh so sweet...spicy. And her body in his arms had felt perfect, like she was meant to be there. Hell, even now, knowing it was best for her if he stayed far, far away, he longed to touch her again.

He ought to leave, just pack up his things and disappear. But he would never—*could never*—do that, knowing she was close to having her child. She needed his help. More than that, even though he knew he would have to leave in the end, and it was going to hurt worse than any of his physical injuries ever had, he craved this time with her — all the time he could have. He wouldn't kiss her again, but he would store up other memories — her smile as she handed him a bowl of ice cream, knowing how much he enjoyed it, her peals of laughter as he told one of the tamer jokes he'd heard from the other guys in his unit, the burning awareness he felt when he caught her looking at him as if she were stealthy. It was as hot as it was adorable that she thought he didn't notice. And if he flexed a little and pretended not to so she'd keep doing it, that was no one's business but his own.

He would hoard those little gems like a miser, storing them up to hold close one day when he was alone again. His chest tightened at the thought, but he tamped down his emotions. He was beginning to care for Clara, more than he'd even known was still possible for a beat-up old jarhead like him. But bad things had happened to people he cared about. He wouldn't be able to stand it if anything happened to harm or change his Clara.

He just had to stop letting his feelings make him an idiot. *Easier said than done*, he thought wryly. He limped back out and finished chopping the pile of wood he'd been working on. His movements were merciless, punishing, until he knew he'd feel it later. But the thought of his Clara Belle crying was all he needed to keep going. He deserved the pain.

Chapter Six

Clara sat on the end of the dock, thinking. She wished she could lie back but she feared she'd never be able to sit up again with her seemingly giant belly and clumsy limbs. Like a turtle on its back, she'd just have to flail and yell for help — or maybe more like a beached whale. Her own thoughts made her laugh aloud. The laughter was a little watery through her tears, but it still felt good. She needed something to cut through the disappointment she was feeling. Disproportionate, really, considering she hadn't even known Fitz that long, but he was special. She knew that much.

Stroking the weathered wood of the old dock, built by her grandfather and refinished by her and her brother last year, centered her. It was a little rough in places, had been beaten up, but it had been smoothed by time and love. *Family.* It seemed like Fitz might need a little smoothing, too. And he'd actually said quite a bit about himself. Revealed some of the pain he'd kept so tightly bottled.

She'd grown to care for him—maybe even more than care for him—over the past days they'd spent together. Beyond that, she wanted to help him—to help bear and lighten the terrible burden he carried. Heaven knew she could understand feeling guilty. Her own guilt gnawed at the pit of her stomach almost daily. How had she been so stupid with Brock? What kind of life would it be for her child without a father? Worse, she knew there had been time she'd spent with her ex—*wasted* on him—that she'd never get back—time she could have been spending with her family or friends, with people who genuinely cared for her.

Her concerns paled in comparison to Fitz's, though. His words rang loud in her ears. "*I miscalculated on my last mission. Badly. It cost my division heavily. Really severe injuries and one...casualty.*" She'd seen the evidence of the physical ramifications on Fitz, and her heart went out to the others who'd been injured. And the soldier who'd been killed—how horrible. How tragic. But she didn't believe Fitz could have caused that tragedy, at least not in any way but through a terrible accident. It was obvious that he'd nearly been a second casualty, with how extensive his own wounds had been. No matter how things stood between them, she was determined to learn more and to help him—because living weighed down with guilt was crushing him.

She had a weird moment on her way back up the path toward the house. She heard something heavy fall to the ground, then rustling, so that she froze in place. She nearly screamed for Fitz, stopped only by how mortified she would feel if it turned out to be nothing. The sound didn't come again, but she still felt uneasy, and the goosebumps that had risen on her arms prickled as she hurried back toward the safety of the cabin—and of Fitz.

He was just finishing up the wood when she waddled past him to return to the house, still rubbing her arms. As soon as she saw him, calm and steady as he finished chopping the pile of wood, she felt silly for her wild imaginings. He'd even managed to stack the split logs neatly into the wheelbarrow. Lars would carry it into the house the next day when he came by, since Fitz still couldn't manage something so heavy.

That afternoon, true to their discussion, they carried on as if the little interlude earlier had never happened. She started on supper, and he filled the sunshower contraption she had rigged up. Too bad it wouldn't work for much longer when the weather turned cold. She supposed she'd have to heat water for a bath then—or just do sponge baths. *Yikes.* She'd never spent a winter out at the cabin, but she wasn't about to give in and stay with Lars. He'd just about stopped asking since she'd been so firm on it, but if she showed any sign of wavering, she knew her brother would be right back to begging her to come stay in his house, where he could help her.

Clara wasn't sure why she was being so stubborn, but she just knew that she had to be on her own. Only Fitz's presence didn't bother her somehow. It didn't sting her pride and make her feel dependent. She never felt like she was conceding anything when she let him help her with things. Maybe because it was clear they were both just barely holding themselves together, sometimes with great difficulty.

Standing in the cozy little kitchen where she had made so many happy memories with her grandparents, she chopped the last head of lettuce and tomatoes, and grated cheese for the homemade macaroni and cheese casserole she planned for their supper. It had been the only option, given how barren the shelves and fridge were becoming. They'd have to go into town the next day if they wanted any meals after breakfast. She frowned at the realization. How the heck had they gone through her supplies so quickly? It was almost as if things were disappearing off the shelves, and she could have sworn that the bottle containing the baby aspirin she had to take every day to prevent her blood pressure from creeping up had moved when neither she nor Fitz had been in the kitchen. She'd had to chalk it up to mommy-to-be brain, and of course, a pregnant woman and a big former Marine weren't exactly light eaters. Tonight's dinner would be delicious, though.

As she looked up from her work, she could see Fitz limping from the water pump to the makeshift shower shed. The muscles in his arms and back rippled as he carried small buckets to fill the tanks. He looked large, strong and rugged, with stubborn determination in every movement. Good heavens, he was gorgeous, and so sexy her mouth went dry. When she realized she was ogling him again, she mentally kicked herself. It wasn't easy, but she dragged her eyes away from his powerful frame and back to her work.

He came in for dinner around six o'clock, exactly the same time he'd been coming in every night. She was mystified by how he could know the time so perfectly, since he didn't wear a watch, but she figured he must be good at reading the position of the sun. He smiled at her a little warily.

"Something smells good." He sniffed appreciatively and the kitchen chair creaked as he lowered himself onto it. Although the pose was relaxed enough, she could still see tension in his limbs.

"Macaroni and cheese casserole. It's cooling now and should be ready to eat in another five minutes or so. I've got salad to start with, though."

Fitz visibly relaxed when he realized she still wasn't going to say anything about earlier, either. "Sounds great," he said, taking the bowl she handed him and crunching into a tomato without delay.

"I love the stuff you put on your salads... What is it?" he asked around a mouthful.

"Dressing?" she couldn't help teasing.

He made a face. "Of course, but it's sure as heck not the Italian or Ranch we got in the Corps."

Clara loved that he'd noticed, way more than she should have, but tried not to let her pleasure show. "I make it myself. It's olive oil, shallot vinegar, mustard, a pinch of salt and some minced herbs from the garden."

"Well, damned if it isn't better than..." He paused and looked awkward for a second, as if he'd swallowed a bug. "Better than any I've ever tasted," he finished at last. Despite the awkwardness, the compliment sounded genuine.

The corners of her mouth rose almost of their own volition. "I find the fresh herbs really do make a difference."

They passed most of the meal in companionable silence. Clara continued to have bouts where she was just ravenous, then other times where she felt her belly was too full of baby to even drink much water. Fitz seemed content to focus mostly on his food, only pausing occasionally to marvel at the obvious movements of her stomach.

"Wow, he or she is moving a heck of a lot. That's normal, right?"

Clara laughed and grimaced simultaneously as another internal assault began. She swore she could feel her baby's rear end move from one side of her stomach to the other as she was kicked in the ribs in the process. "Definitely normal — especially for my little guy or gal. This baby has always been really active, only now there's not much space, and this one doesn't seem to like being slowed down. These days, I'm more worried when I'm not feeling movements. Gosh, Baby Olafson even had the hiccups last week for an hour." Cara grinned at the memory. "I called Lars in the middle of the night because the movements were so regular and I just...didn't know what to make of it. He rushed over and listened with his mobile fetal monitor and, yep, hiccups. I get them a lot too, when I'm excited."

Fitz's rusty chuckle rolled into the small kitchen, filling the room, and his face looked suddenly younger. Lighter. "I never knew babies could get the hiccups. That's incredible."

"Me neither, but boy do I know now." Clara smiled. "Lars teased me mercilessly — would still be teasing me, actually, if you weren't here, so I should thank you for saving me from it. But he was just as concerned as I was, and he ought to know better, O great and powerful doctor that he is."

Fitz looked as though a question was burning on the tip of his tongue, but he wasn't going to ask it. It looked painful, that curiosity, and Clara took pity on him.

"Oh, go on." Clara sighed. "Whatever it is, you can ask it."

The shock on his face was comical, as if she had read his mind.

"How — ?" he spluttered.

"Oh, what, because you're a big, bad Marine I'm not supposed to be able to tell when you're nearly dying of curiosity?" She raised her eyebrows.

Fitz tried to look stern but his eyes twinkled with mirth. "First, I *am* a very big, and *extremely* bad Marine." His mouth twitched. "Second, no, you are not supposed to notice. The KGB, CIA and FBI have got nothing on Clara Olafson's interrogation skills."

Clara chuckled. She couldn't help it. She enjoyed seeing this playful side of him so much. "Be afraid, be *very* afraid." She narrowed her eyes and pursed her lips in her best tough guy impression.

Fitz's answering bark of laughter was loud in the quiet evening, but he didn't speak. The question still hung suspended in the air, unspoken but unmistakable.

"Go on. Don't make me beat it out of you. Tickle torture is my specialty. Just ask my brother."

Fitz's sigh was put-upon but good-natured. "All right. Just remember, you asked for it. I wondered why you decided not to find out if it was a girl or a boy."

Clara's intuition told her that wasn't the question that had had him hesitating, but she decided to play along. "That's an easy one. I like surprises." She paused to think about it. "Nice surprises, anyway," she amended. "And what could possibly be a nicer surprise than meeting my little boy or girl?" She took a sip of lime seltzer water. "It's the same for names. I've thought about them a bit, but not too much. I want to look at him or her then I think I'll just know."

She sat back in her chair and fixed her gaze on Fitz. "Nice try, soldier, but that wasn't the question that had you hesitating, was it?"

Fitz put his finger in the collar of his T-shirt as if it were suddenly too tight. "I don't want to offend you..."

"Unlikely. I mean, it's possible, sure, but I'm an unmarried pregnant woman living in her own very small hometown. I've heard just about everything already." When Fitz looked shocked, then furious, she hastened to add. "Oh, not directly. We don't ever like to say anything unkind directly around these parts. But I've heard the rumors. *'That Olafson girl went to the big city and came back alone and pregnant...no ring. We don't even see her in church anymore, and no wonder, dontcha know?'* So don't worry."

A smile played on his lips as she mimicked the voices, with a spot-on heavy Minnesotan accent. "All right," he conceded reluctantly, taking a deep breath. "You called your child Baby Olafson...so I wondered why you weren't using the baby's father's name. But just because I'm asking, you shouldn't feel you have to tell me."

"I know I don't have to tell you, Fitz, but I think I want to. It's pretty simple, too, really. My baby's father doesn't want anything at all to do with either one of us...*ever.*" The pain of the words and the memories behind them still cut her from the inside out. But somehow the hurt wasn't as awful as it had been when she'd sealed it away months earlier. The sympathy on Fitz's face almost made her lose her composure. Funny, in the face of scorn and pity she could remain strong and proud, but when this man looked at her as though knew what the words had cost her and how much sadness was hidden behind them, she could hardly keep herself from crying.

"Honey, I'm so sorry." He took her soft hands into his larger ones and held her gaze for a long moment.

She had the uncomfortable sensation that he saw everything—the raw pain, the initial disbelief at Brock's reaction as she held out hope he'd come around, ending when Brock had made himself totally clear.

"Sometimes, when a man sees his child—"

"*No*," Clara interrupted. "That's not going to happen. He never wants to see our child." Her voice hitched a little and wobbled, but she pulled it together. "At first, he wanted a paternity test."

"*What*? He thought *you* would lie?" Fitz looked shocked, and incensed, his muscles tensing as if he would get up and go after Brock immediately.

Clara turned to look at something else, anything else, since she wasn't sure she could continue if she looked at him. Her eyes settled on the old sink. "Then he changed his mind."

"Idiot came to his senses, then." Fitz's words were gruff.

"No." Clara shook her head. "He decided it didn't matter whether the baby was his. Which it was, of course...biologically, anyway. He'd been urging me to terminate the pregnancy. Forcefully. He even had his attorneys working on putting together some sort of case against me. When I continued to refuse, he proposed a compromise. In documents to be kept under seal, he would sign over all rights to our child to me, never naming himself as the father. He will never see the baby, he owes the baby no financial support and our child is fully my responsibility."

"How could he do that?" Fitz asked. She wasn't sure if he was asking on an emotional or a legal level, but she decided to address the legal specifics.

"It's not simple, usually, but because I agreed, and he has an excellent team of attorneys. The agreement's fully legal and binding." She looked at Fitz when she continued, suddenly wanting to explain, needing to tell him something she hadn't even told her brother. "I never wanted money from Brock. Love and trust...that's what I wanted. At least, in the beginning." Her voice hitched again and she lifted her chin, taking a deep breath. "When he ended our relationship, then I just wanted respect. Then finally, after all the intimidation and urging, late-night phone calls and random visits, at the end of the day, I wanted to be left alone — for my baby and me to be safe."

Fitz's expression was thunderous, with his dark brows drawn together low over his eyes. She hastened to continue. "He never threatened me — not in so many words — but he told me he didn't want his family finding out about our child. His family is wealthy and powerful, and he's their shining star. I just... I was afraid. This was the only way to protect my child. And frankly, I don't want him or her to grow up with any knowledge of a father who didn't care enough to be part of our lives. Anything is better than that."

The tension hung heavy in the room after Clara stopped speaking. The sounds of the crickets and the frogs, mingled with the wind through the leaves of the large trees, drifted in through the open screen door. Fitz had the stray thought that it was probably getting too cold to leave the door and windows open much longer, but the breeze felt nice.

Stunned. That was how he felt about what she'd revealed. He'd known the end of her relationship with her baby's father must have been painful to leave her totally alone in the middle of the woods and so sad while expecting, but he hadn't been prepared for the ugliness she'd described. Her description had been carefully worded, but he'd heard the depth of sadness, disappointment and fear in what she hadn't said.

She hadn't needed to spell it out. The man who'd had the extreme good fortune to hold the affections of this gorgeous, vibrant woman, to hold her sexy body against his and to and to create a life with her, had cast her aside like so much garbage. He was clearly an imbecile. *Brock*, she'd called him. He guessed that she probably hadn't meant to even reveal that much. Fitz had never hated someone based on their name before, but he hated that name now.

Beyond that, what she'd said about her ex's forceful urging for her to end the pregnancy was appalling. That was her choice. Fitz's huge fists clenched involuntarily. There was young and arrogant, which this Brock certainly was to think he could ever find a woman better than Clara. Fitz could understand young and arrogant, the allure of being a rich playboy nobody wanted to say no to. Hell, he'd *been* that. But he'd always been careful that he and his partners were safe. He'd never led them on. He didn't fool himself that he hadn't broken some hearts, but if he had somehow gotten someone pregnant, he would have done the right thing and cared for the baby — tried to care for the mother. How could someone deny his own flesh and blood so entirely? It was almost beyond Fitz's comprehension. Of course, he knew that he'd been changed by the Corps, by what he had seen. He understood the value of human life more — of friendship and loyalty. Love was precious.

The pounding of his heart was making his temple throb as well, and he took a deep breath to get his wild emotions under control. When the hell had he, legendary in his unit for his calm control, become so damn passionate? The answer was right in front of him, of course, staring at him through those large, honest hazel eyes. She looked wary, the obvious pain of the retelling still fresh under her skin, but trusting him. Brock was an out-and-out idiot and a real ass to boot, but he was gone. Because he was gone, Fitz was there. Clara had trusted him with the ugly, painful truth of her past, and he owed her his honest reaction.

"You're a wonderful mother, Clara Belle, even before you've met your baby." Her eyes went suspiciously shiny at the sincerity behind his words.

"Your ex, Brock...well, he's a piece of work. I can't promise I'd be polite if I saw him, knowing how he treated you and Baby O—" Fitz couldn't help growling, but was stopped by the touch of Clara's soft fingers on his face. As always, her touch was electric, waking all of his nerves at once, sometimes painfully, and making him *feel*.

"Thank you," she said simply, and he heard the finality in her tone. She was through discussing the subject for the moment, and he could understand that.

"I have to head into town tomorrow for supplies." She bit her lower lip in a gesture that he was coming to find endearing and unexpectedly sexy. "Especially baby aspirin to keep my blood pressure in check. Even though I thought I had plenty, I can't find my spare bottle and I think that the current bottle might have gone off or something. It's been leaving a funny taste in my mouth all week." Her eyes looked troubled, and he felt a stirring of unease deep in his gut.

85

"I don't like the sound of that. Maybe we should go in tonight."

A crinkle appeared between her russet eyebrows but she shook her head. "No, no…I think tomorrow should be fine. I mean, I have definitely heard that pregnant women can start finding that certain things change taste to them, although I thought that was mostly supposed to be in the first trimester. It's more that I'll feel better if I *know* it's a brand-new bottle, but I should be okay. It's crazy, but my blood pressure has been the exact same every time I've taken it recently — like, no variation at all for almost a week."

Fitz knew that what she said was reasonable, and she obviously didn't want to make a big deal, but he vowed to watch her more closely. "Okay, honey. It's good that it's steady, at least, but maybe we should go early?"

Clara's expression was relieved. "I'd ask if you wanted to stay here and rest, but I think I already know the answer."

His nod was terse. Damn right he wouldn't stay here laying around when she bumped her way back into town and hauled heavy groceries alone. "I'm coming."

"That's what I thought you'd say," she said, sounding resigned but not altogether displeased. Amusement crept into her tone at her next words. "I have an ulterior motive, too. Tonight's ice cream will be the last if we don't stop in at the grocery store, and you *do not* want to see me with fireball heartburn and no ice cream in the house if I don't have enough hands to carry all my bags." She got up as she spoke, turning her back to him and scooping ice cream into two bowls.

He admired the curve of her back and her lush derrière in stretch pants almost unconsciously and had to drag his eyes away, reminding himself he had no right. Even if the memory of how amazing she'd felt against him, in his arms, on his lap, seemed burned into his very skin.

"We can't have that," he answered lightly, going along with the abrupt change of subject as he accepted one bowl from her. He understood. Revealing so much could leave a person raw, exposed. He was in awe of her courage, trusting him, especially after he'd lost control and how he'd acted toward her earlier. He knew he didn't have a hope of being good enough for her, but damn if he didn't wish he could be with every fiber of his body and soul. It was as if, in her, he'd found the dream he'd always fought for, fought to protect. But he should just be grateful he had the chance to be there for her in such difficult circumstances.

"And you're right, honey," he added. "I don't need the rest, but I do need to be there to help you carry everything."

He wasn't speaking only about the groceries. He saw that she understood from the flicker in her eyes, but she didn't say anything about it.

They finished their dessert with only light conversation and went to bed, where he tossed and turned, restless, as always. For once, the dreams that tormented him weren't of the fire and the desert, but instead of the generous curves, soft hair and skin, and sweet mouth that he longed to hold and possess again and again.

Chapter Seven

Fitz woke up as grumpy as a bear with a sore tooth, and Clara thought he probably *had* strained his knee the day before with the wood or carrying water, even though she knew he'd never admit it. His eyes were bloodshot again, as if he hadn't slept well, and even his short hair had somehow managed to get rumpled. He still looked like sin on two legs, though, and somehow it just made him all the more ruggedly handsome.

A memory of Brock popped into her head, unbidden. Her ex-boyfriend hadn't been a morning person, and he liked to shower, shave, dress and have coffee before speaking to another soul. On one of the rare occasions that she'd spent the whole night at his place, since he'd never wanted to spend much time at her apartment, she'd tried to playfully seduce him in the morning. He'd completely snapped at her and stomped away, leaving her feeling naked and vulnerable, alone in bed. The memory still stung.

When Clara looked at Fitz, even though he was obviously out of sorts, his eyes and face remained somehow gentle. Even though his replies were a little short, nothing he said was malicious. The contrast between the two men was so stark that she couldn't believe she had ever thought the way Brock acted was normal. Hard-earned wisdom, she supposed.

"All right, Sergeant Sunshine. Let's head on into the big city of Cameronville," she said.

Fitz's tight smile was more of a grimace.

"Are you...? Is your leg up to this?" she probed gently.

The glower he turned on her should have set her hair on fire, but his eyes gentled before he spoke. "It's... I took some medicine, so it should feel better soon," he conceded. "Sorry for the attitude, *ma'am*."

It was definitely a term of endearment this time. As the ghost of dimple flashed on his cheek with his small smile, her heart squeezed. *How the heck is he so gosh darn charming?*

"Apology accepted," she said, stopping herself from saying anything more by heading out to the truck, only to halt in her tracks as she opened the door to her shiny, black pick-up and tried to figure out how she was going to climb in. She loved trucks. She'd almost always driven trucks, even in the city. They were just so big and useful. However, as her pregnancy had progressed, it had gotten harder and harder to clamber up into the seat. Now, two weeks after her last trip into town, she feared she'd finally hit her limit. She lifted her leg, leaning against the doorjamb. To her horror, her foot barely made it halfway to the step before stopping. Her stomach sank and felt like the bottom dropped right out of it.

"Oh, *crud*," she breathed out.

Any thought that she'd been sneaky enough for Fitz to miss what she'd done was shattered when she felt his solid, warm presence at her elbow. Despite how she kept trying to tell her hormones to stop paying so much attention to Fitz, she still felt a flutter in her belly and a thrill roll from her toes to her fingertips at his nearness.

"I'm fine," she lied.

Silence was the only response. *Wise, wise man*, she thought. She leaned forward and put her elbows on the floor of the cab, managing to get a knee onto the bottom step — where she promptly floundered. Frustration filled her, and she felt her cheeks go hot and prickly with a blush and sheer cussedness.

"Ah, honey..." Fitz began tentatively. She would have been amused at the trepidation she saw on his face — the hulking retired Marine was afraid of little old her — but she was too darned angry and flustered.

"All right," she snapped with poor grace. "I'll let you help, even though I don't need it." She felt bad about her nasty tone, even as the words were still leaving her mouth, but she couldn't help them. It was as if a mean, wet hen had taken over her body.

Fitz's mouth twitched as if he were fighting a smile at her outrageous statement, and he boosted her up into the seat seemingly without effort, putting his large hands right onto her curvy bottom and pushing. His wrist had been healing beautifully and was now pretty much back to normal, but she hoped this wouldn't set back any of that recovery. She could feel the warmth of his large hands through the thin, soft material of her pants. If they lingered a second or two longer than they needed to, she wasn't going to complain, although Fitz looked a little guilty when she looked down at him.

"Thanks," she said, but she wasn't sure if she actually achieved the gracious tone she'd intended. His swift smile made his eyes crinkle at the corners, and he lowered his gaze to her feet. They'd seemed particularly swollen this morning, but she'd been too proud to ask for his help with her socks, so she wore only sandals—loosely fastened, at that.

He thrust his hands into his pockets, and her breath caught in her throat when she saw what he pulled out of them. Fuzzy, warm socks with little rainbows on them. *Her* socks, from the clean laundry basket.

With tender hands that cradled her feet as if they were precious, he undid her sandals, put on her socks and slid her shoes back on.

"There you go, honey," he said gruffly, patting her left foot a little awkwardly. She was touched, warmed from the inside out, that in spite of his own pain, he'd been so thoughtful.

"Thank you," she breathed.

His bright blue eyes were fathomless as their gazes locked, and thoughts and emotions swirled in their depths, but tenderness and affection were obvious. He looked away first, seeming uncomfortable at having revealed himself. He shut the door and limped around to the passenger seat, jumping up as if he'd had a lot of practice getting into high vehicles, even with an injury—which, she supposed, he probably had. There was so much more she wanted to know about him, but for now, everything she knew was enough.

One thing was clear, though. The prior afternoon might have been the close of a Chapter of their book but the rest of the novel, including the ending, was still to come. The engine roared to life as she turned the key and they bumped their way into town on the pothole-covered gravel roads.

Cameronville was the biggest town for over a hundred miles in every direction as well as the county seat, but that really wasn't saying much when the entire county only had about ten thousand residents. It had a stoplight, though, and they were up to three four-way stop signs. Lars had medical offices there, though he was hardly ever in them. There were a couple of pretty little prairie churches — Lutheran, of course — and two diners, which catered a lot to tourists in the summer and were much quieter and strictly for locals in the winter. There were still groups of tourists heading through on their way to fish or canoe in the parks farther north, but the groups were dwindling as the summer wound to a close. They drove past a couple of faces she didn't recognize, but for the most part, every single person they passed was someone she'd known for as long as she could remember. She waved and smiled at everyone, strangers included, as they drove the two blocks of Main Street, past the library and the sporting goods store, the bakery and the one bar, finally pulling into the small grocery store parking lot.

"Do you know all those people?" Fitz's voice was incredulous.

She shrugged. "Most of them, yeah. But we wave at everyone around here."

"Even from your car?" Fitz asked.

"Oh, yeah. From the car, on the street, everywhere. People are super nice." She laughed. "You should see us at the four-way stop signs. I think that's why they put in the stoplight, actually. Everyone kept waving to everyone else to go first, and it was causing traffic jams. I try to avoid Cameron Street from four until five o'clock. There's not much traffic, but it can get backed up from sheer Minnesota politeness."

"Pretty different from the Twin Cities," Fitz observed dryly.

"Oh, have you spent some time there, then?" she asked curiously, and he looked uncomfortable. He was saved from answering by a tapping on her window. She looked over into the light blue eyes of her best friend, Amber.

Amber beamed with surprised pleasure, and she opened the truck door, reaching in to hug Clara and engulfing her in the rose-scented perfume she'd favored since junior high. When she pulled back and noticed Fitz, her eyes narrowed.

"I *thought* that was your truck, but I didn't think you were coming into town for another week or so?" Amber made the statement a question, studying Fitz openly as she spoke.

"We, uh, needed supplies," Clara explained lamely.

"I'll *bet* you did," Amber answered, winking just at Clara, but quickly amended, "My little niece or nephew is a growing baby, *aren't you*?" She spoke to Clara's belly, and patted it for good measure.

Clara laughed. "Baby O is definitely growing. Every time I think I can't possibly expand any more, this little one proves me wrong."

Fitz looked confused. "Oh, are you Clara and Lars' sister?" he asked, his eyes going back and forth between them.

If he was searching for physical similarities, Clara knew he wouldn't find them. Where she was small and sturdy, with frizzy reddish hair and hazel eyes, Amber was tall and statuesque, a true Nordic beauty. It was unbelievable that she'd had a child then practically no time later had regained her trim waist and athletic frame. Clara might be jealous if she didn't love the other woman so much and know that she was just as kind inside as she appeared to be on the outside.

"Only by choice, but not by blood," Amber answered, her wide smile showing her bright, even teeth. "You must be the Marine."

"Retired Marine," Fitz corrected. "And word travels fast, huh?"

Clara laid a soothing hand on his left thigh, keeping the pressure light. "No, I only told Lars and Amber about you. No one else knows anything, although, of course, they'll see you today."

Fitz looked mollified by her statement.

She turned toward Amber again. "And I *did* tell you his name was Fitz."

Amber looked suitably chastised. "Yes, and I don't mean to be unfriendly. It's just... We worry about you. But I'm pleased to meet you, Fitz, and I *am* happy there's someone out there with her now." Amber held out her hand and Fitz shook it firmly. "Oops, sorry, forgot to introduce myself. Amber Hanson...best friend, honorary sister and future aunt."

"Nice to meet you, too, Ms. Hanson," Fitz replied. Clara was secretly pleased to notice that, while his face was friendly enough, there was none of the interest or spark in his expression that she saw when he looked at her. He'd reverted to the guarded and stoic expression that seemed to be his default—except around her.

Amber helped her out of the truck's cab, and Fitz came around, walking slowly so that he disguised his limp almost entirely.

"I just finished my shopping and was heading back home." Amber waved vaguely toward her red Chevy, which was worn and dusty. "I really wish I could stay, but Bea's home with Jim and his shift starts at noon. She's going to be *so* disappointed she missed seeing Auntie Clara."

"Bea is Amber's four-year-old daughter," Clara explained to Fitz, then turned back to Amber. "Tell her that I was sorry not to see her, and you both should come out to the cabin again soon."

Amber addressed both of them but seemed to look squarely at Fitz as she spoke. "I might just do that." She eyed Clara's stomach. "I don't think you have much longer to go, Clare."

"A few more weeks, we think. As Lars told me, you can't rush perfection." Clara laughed, but Amber looked dubious.

"Well, as long as you're feeling fine?" Amber's sky-blue eyes were concerned.

"Totally fine. And Fitz has been making sure I don't do too much," Clara reassured her friend. She saw from the corner of her eye that Fitz liked her comment.

"All right then, but you know you can call or text me or Jim anytime, right?" Amber leaned in again, enveloping Clara in her comforting scent as well as her hug once more.

"Of course!" Clara answered.

"Okay," Amber said. "Bye, Fitz. You treat our girl right, okay?" She leaned down to talk to Clara's stomach. "And bye, Baby O. Can't wait to meet you, little one." Tears prickled in Clara's eyes at the real affection she heard in Amber's voice.

Amber strode back to her truck, her long legs eating up the ground rapidly so she was there in no time, and she waved as she drove off, obviously hurrying to get home in time for Jim to leave for work. He was currently a second-shift manager at the local mill, and they'd known him since they'd been in preschool. Amber and Jim had been an item since seventh grade and married since they'd been twenty-two. Clara knew they wished they had more children, but Amber always said that she was and always would be grateful, even if the Good Lord only gave them little Bea.

Fitz's large, reassuring presence at her side pulled her back from her musings to the present.

"Is it wrong that, while I like your brother and your best friend, I also find them terrifying?" Fitz lifted one dark eyebrow quizzically.

Clara couldn't help the laughter that erupted at his comical expression. "I don't believe you, but they would think it was nice of you to notice."

"It's a blow to man's pride, darlin', when he spends his whole career training to be dangerous, has it on good authority that he looks and is, indeed, dangerous, only to have several residents of one tiny Minnesota town completely discount that awesome danger."

A full-body laugh shook Clara's frame, starting low in her stomach, at Fitz's description and delivery. He smiled in return, the genuine smile that made all her senses go on high alert, and he looked relaxed...happy.

"I'm so sorry, Major Menacing. I'll try to get the next people you meet to be appropriately horrified, okay?" she teased as they walked into the small store. It was only when she went to get a cart that she realized he wasn't following her. Turning, she saw him frozen just inside the door, looking at an older couple who had stopped and were staring at him in return. *The Larsons*, she thought, who had three sons.

The expression on Fitz's face was strange, almost as if he'd seen a ghost, but not quite. All his amusement had evaporated, replaced by shock, guilt and a terrible, infinite sadness. His eyes seemed to sink a little in his face, and little lines of pain bracketed his lips. She let go of the cart she'd been about to take out and hurried to him, taking his unresisting hand and sidling up next to him, wanting to lend him her strength — all her support.

She turned her gaze to the Larsons, puzzled by what had caused his reaction. Maybe they looked like someone he'd known? But they looked odd, too. Their faces held none of the guilt that Fitz's did, but they looked surprised, sad and even more unexpectedly, *eager*. Mrs. Larson's eyes had filled with tears, but the corners of her mouth turned up in an unmistakable smile of welcome.

"Master Sergeant Fitzhugh?" she asked, then shook her head, rolling her eyes. "What a silly question, of course I can see that it's you. You look just like your pictures and your video chat self. I'm just so surprised to see you in our little town! Gosh, right in the middle of Sav-a-Coin." She turned to her husband. "Lou, you remember Master Sergeant Fitzhugh, don't you? Abraham always talked about him." She turned her earnest, kind face back toward Fitz. "He thought the world of you, you know?"

When Clara glanced up, Fitz still looked frozen, and his blue eyes looked haunted. She thought for a second that he might turn around and just walk right out, but instead he straightened his spine, squared his shoulders and lifted his chin, looking every inch the proud Marine. She squeezed his hand, and he gripped hers so hard that she thought her bones might crack, but she didn't care. Whatever was going on, he knew she was there for him. That was enough.

"I thought the world of him, too, Mrs. Larson. He was a fine soldier…the very finest."

Mrs. Larson's light eyes, which had begun to clear, went shiny again, but her pleasure was obvious. Mr. Larson looked proud as well.

"Thank you, son. That's very kind of you to say so. Most kind." His eyes were suspiciously bright as well, and his mustache fluttered with the force of his words and his nodding. He looked at his wife. "And of course, I remember hearing about Master Sergeant Fitzhugh, Martha." He turned back to Fitz and his eyes held a depth of gratitude. "We got your letter, son. It meant a lot, especially because we heard how badly you were injured, braving the fire and getting burned yourself."

Someone passed by them, staring curiously.

"Would you like to come over for some cocoa and brownies? We only live a couple of blocks away. I know it's still summer, but my goodness, I think it feels like cocoa weather already. I said to myself this morning, '*Martha, you'd better make sure you have cocoa ready in case the boys come home*.'" Her tone was light, but Clara could see hope in every nuance of her expression.

"Martha, dear, I think these young people probably have shopping to do. We shouldn't keep them." Lou Larson's words gave them a clear opportunity to escape, but his eyes contradicted his words. He hoped they would come, maybe even more than his wife did.

Clara felt like she was part of a play where everyone else knew their lines and the plot, and she didn't even have a script. It was disconcerting. She looked at Fitz — at his proud, handsome face, so filled with agony at this chance meeting. Then the pieces clicked together, and her heart swelled in her chest with sympathy, empathy, for all of them.

She remembered that there had been a memorial not long before she'd come home for a local boy, a Marine, killed in Afghanistan. *Abraham Larson.*

When Fitz looked down at her, his soul was raw, right there underneath the surface of his eyes. She didn't want to say it out loud, but she wanted him to know that whatever he decided, she would be fine with it. If it was better to leave for now, that was okay, and she'd go with him. But if he wanted to stay, and go with the Larsons, she'd be there with him every step of the way. She laid her free hand on his arm, and continued to hold his hand, leaning in so close she could smell his spicy scent.

She saw his decision before he said anything.

"If we can come back in a little bit for our supplies, I think we'd be honored to join you for a while." Mr. and Mrs. Larson both flushed with pleasure, and Clara felt nothing but pride and admiration for this brave man she'd had the honor to get to know. She knew how difficult it had to be and how much it would cost him, but none of that shone on his face.

"Of course. We can certainly come back later," Clara agreed.

They walked with the Larsons to their house, which was just as close as they'd said, right off Main Street. Fitz walked carefully, and if she hadn't known about his injury, she never would have suspected. The house was painted light blue, very cozy-looking, complete with flower beds and a white picket fence. There was a well-used basketball hoop mounted on their garage. Clara could imagine that it must have gotten a lot of use with three boys.

When they walked in, they were ushered directly to the living room couch by Mrs. Larson. The place smelled sweet and warm, like something baking. The living room was neat, and although none of the furniture looked new, it was carefully kept. All around the room were pictures, hanging on the walls and sitting on the fireplace mantel, of lively young boys gradually changing into handsome young men. In the very center of the mantel sat a framed picture of the young Marine who must have been Abraham Larson, and above it they had mounted his folded-up flag, the flag from his funeral.

Mrs. Larson bustled into the kitchen, but Mr. Larson lingered for a moment longer. "Can I get you two anything else besides cocoa and brownies? Pop, water or milk?"

"Milk would be wonderful for me, thanks," Clara answered.

Fitz didn't appear to have heard. He was staring so intently at the picture. He still held her hand, but he seemed a million miles away. Mr. Larson didn't seem offended, though, and followed his wife into the kitchen where she could hear the faint clink of dishes.

When they were alone, she put her hand on Fitz's thigh. He started, jumping a little under her touch. The look he turned on her was torn...agonized.

"I thought I could do this. Damn, I came here, to Cameronville, partly *to* do this. But now, ah, Clara Belle, I don't know if I can."

"I say do whatever you can, then we leave, no questions. I honestly think these people will understand, maybe better than anyone else, if you can't stay. What you've already done has clearly meant a lot to them." Clara kept her voice low, and she leaned closer so only Fitz would hear her.

He closed his eyes, and when he opened them, they were less haunted…less like an animal caught in a steel trap. He took her hands into both of his and searched her eyes as he spoke. "I don't know what in the hell I ever did to deserve your kindness, honey, and to have you believe in me the way you do, but I don't know that I care right now. Just…it means a lot, Clara." His raspy voice was rougher than usual at the end, and it warmed Clara.

"I'm yours," she whispered, immediately embarrassed by what she'd revealed without thinking. Luckily, Mr. Larson had been returning with her milk, and she didn't think Fitz had heard. Or if he had, he hadn't reacted.

Sitting in that warm, cozy living room was one of the hardest things Fitz had ever done. Facing these two kind, gentle souls who'd lost someone incredibly dear to them was his worst nightmare, and he didn't know how he would have gotten through it without Clara. She made him want to be the man she believed he was—a better man. And so, he became that man. For *her. At least for now*, a little voice in his head reminded him, *until she finds out you've been lying to her.*

When they'd all settled into the orange-and-brown woven couches, Clara with her milk and the rest of them with cocoa and brownies, he somehow found the reserves inside of himself to talk about that awful day.

"Mr. and Mrs. Larson, Abe was a hero…a real hero," he started, bracing himself to relive the horror of his last mission so they would understand.

Mr. Larson broke in. "Martha and Lou, son. *Martha and Lou.* And you don't have to tell us anything. That was a fine letter you sent. There's no need for more."

He opened and closed his mouth, completely taken aback by Lou Larson's comment. It was not at all what he'd expected. Fitz barely remembered writing the letter from his hospital bed. Nearly overcome by guilt, with nightmares every night of the promise he couldn't keep, he'd written a long letter expressing his deepest sympathies.

"We don't blame you, dear," Martha added. "We both wanted you to know that, and so did our other sons. We're so glad you're here. It's amazing to see you walking. After we heard how badly you'd been hurt and burned, trying to save Abraham, we worried. We called the hospital every day, then every week, and they told us you were making progress, so we knew you were getting better." She paused and swiped at a tear. "But hearing it isn't the same as seeing it for yourself, is it?"

Her husband took her hand, and they exchanged a look. One of the infinitely intimate understanding looks of people who have been together a long time and have survived.

"They never told me," Fitz said, but it was more of a faint question.

"Oh, *no*. We told them not to. We didn't want to make things harder on you, being reminded of us," Martha answered.

"I...uh, this is...I was going to tell you what really happened," Fitz stammered. He looked at Clara, and her presence was like a cool breeze, calm and peaceful, steadying him. He could practically feel the support and kindness, gentleness and affection, rolling off her in waves.

Lou Larson's voice was gentle. "The Corps told us, son, and you told us. But we already knew that

Abraham was a good man. We miss him every day, but we know that he died doing something he believed in deeply. So, if you don't mind, we'd really like to hear about the other times. The fun times. Maybe how you became friends? And about the other guys in your unit?"

Fitz let out the breath he didn't know he'd been holding, and he looked at Martha Larson for confirmation. She nodded. Clara's hand, still gripped tightly in his, was like an anchor, strong and steady.

"Well, sure. Of course I can talk about that. When I met Abe, he was a skinny little recruit, but what he lacked in muscle, he damn sure made up for in grit and determination..." He shot a guilty look at Martha Larson. "Sorry about the language."

She laughed. "Oh my goodness, bless you if you think I raised three boys without hearing that word before in my house."

Fitz smiled and relaxed a little at her words. "Did you know the other guys nicknamed him Honest Abe?"

Martha shook her head no.

"They told me it was because, in Basic, he was so transparent that he would get them in trouble for even thinking of doing anything wrong. Like, they hadn't even taken extra rations, but his face would look so guilty that they'd still end up being punished." Fitz shook his head with a smile. "But that's the kind of guy you want at your six. I mean, your back. He was someone who really looked out for all the other guys. That's why I usually had him ride with me—to scan and be aware, protecting the group."

"That *is* a very kind thing to say, son," Lou said, and the pleasure on both of their faces was genuine.

They spent over an hour at the Larsons', and he told story after story, making them all laugh. And somewhere in the middle of it, something loosened in his chest, something that had been crushing him. When he looked over at Clara, her pretty face framed with her wild hair, and saw the admiration and trust written there, he felt proud of himself.

Not the way he used to when he was an arrogant ass, self-entitled and superior, secure in the knowledge that his money bought him anything he wanted. No, he felt proud of himself again for being a good soldier in a job that broke a lot of men. He felt proud of himself for being there for Clara when she needed him. He felt proud for bringing joy and peace to a couple who had experienced the worst kind of pain and grief a parent could suffer. It felt really good... *right*.

He was deep into a story that had them all laughing when he heard Clara's stomach give a huge rumble. He hadn't even known stomachs could make noises like that.

"I'm so sorry, baby. You and Baby O must be starving," he apologized.

Clara's answering smile was sheepish. "We're always starving these days, it seems. No worries."

Still, he rose with a snap and winced as a spear of pain shot through his knee at the unexpected activity. "It must be past lunchtime, though, and we still have to get supplies." As Clara got up from the couch, rising in the move that never failed to amaze him since she seemed to lead entirely with her belly, he apologized to the Larsons for cutting off their visit so abruptly.

Martha waved off his apology. "No problem. We understand. You've given us so much, today, young man." Her voice wavered as she spoke, and Lou continued where she left off.

"We can never tell you how grateful we are. Now go on and get your woman some food, son." He winked as he spoke, his mustache waggling, and Clara and Fitz were still laughing as they left.

"Now that you know where to find us, you come back anytime!" Martha called as she and Lou waved from the front door.

Fitz took Clara's hand as they walked. He didn't need the support anymore, but he liked the way it felt. Like they fit together perfectly. His mind wandered into other ways they might fit together, but they reached the store before he could pursue those thoughts much further.

"Seriously, honey, are you okay not eating while we do the shopping?" he asked worriedly. He didn't know that much about pregnant women, but he did know they were hungry. And Clara seemed to get faint if she didn't eat enough or stood too quickly.

"I'm all right, but maybe we could go fast? And get something quick on the way home, too?" she answered.

Fitz didn't like the strain he saw on her face. "Damn it, I'm so sorry. We stayed too long. I should have been watching the time."

The look his little Clara turned on him was fierce. "I was *glad* to be there. And if I had wanted to leave, I would have said so."

She was so lovely when she was prickly. His feisty Clara, with her cheeks flushed and her eyes sparkling.

"We'll go fast then," he said gently. "And, Clara," he added, "I was glad you were there, too."

She lowered her stubborn little chin and her eyes softened. "Well, *good.*"

Chapter Eight

They got through the supermarket at light speed, and Clara had to admit, if only to herself because she certainly wouldn't admit it out loud, it was amazing to have Fitz helping. Even something as simple as reaching to the top of a pile of tomatoes was becoming difficult. And she was feeling so out-of-breath sometimes, just in the past couple of days, with a couple of piercing headaches that had seemed to occur without warning. As Fitz had recovered, she was getting less and less mobile. She knew it was normal for the very late stages of pregnancy but, *jeez*, it didn't make it any easier.

She let Fitz load most of the groceries into the back of the truck, enjoying the view of the thick muscles in his arms and back, and the way his jeans cupped his very fine derriere. She blushed and looked away when she realized what she'd been doing, but his grin as he'd finished told her that he'd noticed.

When she got to the driver's side of the cab, everything in her wanted to at least make a show of getting in on her own, but she'd learned her lesson. There was a fine line between stubborn and stupid. She tried never to cross it, and it would be clearly on the side of stupid not to accept Fitz's help. His face registered surprise when she didn't make the attempt at hoisting herself up.

"Uh-oh, honey. Are you all right?" he teased.

She sighed, blowing the air straight up to dislodge all the little hairs that had escaped her ponytail and stuck to the fine sheen of sweat on her forehead. *Sweat, for heaven's sake!* It was fifty-five degrees out and she was sweating. *Hormones suck. Big time.*

"I'm not so ornery I can't admit when I'm wrong." She thought for a second. "Well, most of the time, anyway," she added with what she hoped was her most winning smile.

Fitz's bark of laughter echoed in the truck cabin as he helped her in with a tenderness she wouldn't have guessed he was capable of when she'd first met him. His large hands lingered again at her waist longer than was strictly necessary and brushed against her rear end as well, but she wasn't complaining. She stole a look at him under her eyelashes and saw a banked desire burning in his eyes to match her own.

It was amazing, but he looked much more relaxed than he had earlier, even when they'd arrived. The visit with the Larsons had done him a lot of good. Oh, the depths of his eyes still held shadows, and pain — and she was beginning to suspect there was some secret he kept dancing around — but some of the guilt had lightened. With his surprise visit and stories, he'd brought the Larsons joy that they wouldn't otherwise have known.

They stopped at Dairy Queen on the way out of town, mostly because she'd practically had to wipe drool off her mouth as soon as she'd seen the sign. Fitz had noticed the unsubtle signs of her ravenous hunger and insisted they pull in, where he got her two cheeseburgers, fries and a milkshake, which she devoured before they left the parking lot. Like the gentleman he was, he didn't comment on the amount of food she'd consumed, but she'd caught him hiding a grin.

Embarrassment made her cheeks hot, and she blurted out the first thought that popped into her head. "Want to see something beautiful?"

The muscles in Fitz's tanned neck worked as he sipped from his soda, and he swallowed before he answered. "I've found a lot of beauty here already, Clara Belle, but I definitely want to see whatever you want to show me." His tone and expression were oddly intimate, alone as they were in the truck. She marveled again at how ridiculously handsome he was. Such an odd contradiction of masculine beauty and toughness, it shouldn't have worked, but boy, did it.

"I thought we'd maybe drive by Cameron's Bluff." She had been thinking no such thing, but now that she pictured it, it felt right. It was picturesque and peaceful—away from the little cabin where they'd briefly felt the flare of such passion, then doused it with cold water.

"Sounds spectacular, if you're sure you're up for it?" Fitz made his statement a question. She loved hearing the concern in his deep, rumbling voice.

"Yeah, I was feeling a little off before lunch, but I think I'm back to normal now." The baby gave a forceful kick as if to agree, making her belly move unmistakably, and they both laughed. "It's so cool out, so none of our groceries should melt if we stop for a bit," she added, thinking out loud.

"All right, then. Drive on, ma'am."

The bluff wasn't far out of town, so they were pulling onto the turn-off practically before she knew it.

"It's a popular spot at night, for the high schoolers to park and, you know, *neck*." She blushed again, cursing her fair complexion, which meant he couldn't fail to notice. "But we should have it ourselves this time of day."

Fitz's chuckle rolled around the small space, to her delight. "Do you have designs on my virtue, Ms. Olafson?" he teased, then paused. "And does *anyone* use the word 'neck' anymore? *Really*? I thought that went out of style with Brylcreem and hot rods."

She pursed her lips. "What do *you* call it?" she asked defensively.

"Making out," he said, reaching a long, muscular arm to rest on the back of her seat. "Kissing until neither one of us can see straight."

Clara's mind flashed back to their kisses from the day before — his taste, the hardness of his body all along the softness of hers, how he'd warmed her with the heat of his body and with the force of their attraction.

She brought the truck to an abrupt stop and clambered down awkwardly before he had a chance to say anything else. "We're here," she announced unnecessarily.

The sound of his door slamming echoed, and he came around more slowly, walking to stand by her side. The glory of the entire river valley, blanketed on either side by tall pine trees, spread out before them. It was one of her favorite sights in the entire world, and she missed it every time she left Cameronville. The air smelled fresh, like pine trees with a hint of autumn and winter to come, and the gurgling of the water over the rocks was soothing. *Utterly peaceful.*

"Glorious. Like a little bit of heaven right here in northern Minnesota."

Fitz's words should have sounded silly, but instead, in that quiet space, just the two of them, they sounded like the truest thing she'd ever heard. Clara was ridiculously pleased that the place had affected him as much as it affected her. When she turned to look at him, she realized he was staring at her instead of at the view. Something in his expression was so exquisitely tender — infinitely lovely — that she felt a warm blush spread from the roots of her hair all over her face, and even prickling onto her chest and arms. It was an intimate look, as if he were fully seeing and understanding her for the first time, and he loved what he saw.

"Thank you for being with me at the Larsons', Clara." His rasping voice was low and intense, but she heard it in spite of the gentle noises surrounding them.

"Of course. Although you didn't need me."

His expression was fierce. "Oh, I needed you, honey. I think I would have turned right around and left the store if you hadn't been next to me. Or I would have run out of their house as soon as I saw Abe's picture, if you hadn't been right there holding my hand."

Clara shook her head vigorously. "Don't underestimate yourself, Fitz."

"How do you that?" His voice was wondering.

"What?" she asked.

"You've seen me. Heard me. I know I'm pretty damn grumpy, with a body that won't always do what I want it to anymore and a mind that isn't much better." He rubbed his hand on the back of his neck and looked away before turning his piercing gaze back on her. "But you look at me like you trust me, believe in me—like I'm still one of the good guys."

"You *are* a good guy," she countered.

"That's what I'm talking about. Right there. I love seeing that look in your beautiful eyes, soft and kinda sparkling. Hearing the conviction in your voice. You make me want to be a better man, baby. The man you seem to see." His words were so sweet her heart thumped in her chest like a drum.

"But that man would know not to choose you, that you deserved so much better—all of the best that this life has to offer." The words sounded torn from him, wrenched from his chest.

Clara reacted before she could think about it. *Darned impulsive nature.* "What if I choose you?" she asked in a quick, breathy voice.

The mix of emotions that flashed across Fitz's face all at once was dizzying—joy and affection, maybe even something more, followed by guilt and, finally, resigned sadness. "That's a beautiful thing to say, Clara Belle."

"We've both known sadness, Fitz. If my past isn't too ugly for you, what makes you think yours will be too ugly for me?" She fixed her eyes on his, trying to convey the depth of feeling she realized she had for this man who'd been a stranger and had now somehow come to mean so much to her.

Honor warred with desire in every line of his body, and Clara knew it was crazy to push him like this. But everything in him called to her. As if all her ragged edges matched up perfectly with his so that together, they were smoothed out. Feeling like she was stepping off the edge of the bluff they stood so near to, she took a step closer so that scant inches separated them.

"Ah, baby," he said, groaning, and covered her mouth with his, pulling her flush against the hard planes of his body. He tasted vaguely of chocolate and his own unique spice, and she drank him in as if she would never get enough. Where their kiss the day before had been passionate, this kiss was explosive. He touched her everywhere, running his hands up and down her back, tangling them in her hair, and finally cupping the swell of her butt, pulling her closer against him. And she reveled in his possession and the closeness. The sensual slide of his tongue against hers, the gentle tugging and nipping of his lips and teeth on her lips made her body come alive. Her nipples beaded against his chest, even through their layers of clothing, and she looped her arms around his neck to hold him closer.

The pleasure—almost blissful—was shattered by a swift, spearing pain in the area of her ribs. It was higher than the baby, and so sharp it felt like she'd been stabbed. With a long sword. At her gasp, Fitz released her, then grabbed her again to steady her when she doubled over in agony.

"Oh *damn, damn, damn.* Honey, I'm so sorry. Did I hurt you?"

She heard his voice, heavy with concern, as if through a long tunnel.

"No...not you," she panted. When she managed to lift her head and squinted up at him, he looked weird. Blurry. She tried closing one eye, then the other, but it didn't help. The wavery image might not be clear, but she could still see the gravity in his face and body language.

"Baby," he said gently, as if trying not to scare her. "I think we need to call your brother. Where's your phone?"

At the total calm and confidence she heard in his voice, her heart stopped pounding so hard and she relaxed a little. Whatever was wrong, Fitz would take care of her.

"In the cup holder," she said, wondering why she felt so out of breath. She suddenly remembered she'd woken up out-of-breath overnight, too.

"Can you walk there, honey, or should I carry you?"

The question was ridiculous. Of course she could walk, and he shouldn't be carrying her or anything heavy. "I'll walk," she answered. But even with his arm steadying her, it suddenly wasn't easy at all.

When Fitz lifted her into the passenger seat, she saw grim determination on his face. The amazing soldier he must have been. *Her* soldier.

He jumped into the driver's seat and grabbed her phone, quickly scrolling to Lars' number and dialing.

"It's Fitz calling you from Clara's phone," Fitz said tersely before the other man would have had a chance to say anything. "We stopped off at Cameron's Bluff but Clara's having sudden pain."

He nodded at whatever Lars said and held out the phone, pressing a button.

"You're on speakerphone now, Lars."

"Clara?" Lars' voice was a little garbled from the cell signal, but comforting nonetheless. "Can you talk?"

"Yeah," she answered. She wanted to sound reassuring, but instead she thought her voice sounded a little weak.

"That's really good. What does the pain feel like? Where is it?" Lars was using the doctor's voice she always made fun of, but now she kind of liked it. It was easier to talk to her doctor than her brother.

She thought carefully before answering. "High. Not my chest, but not near the baby, either. Like in my upper ribs."

"Are you having any swelling? Blurred vision? Shortness of breath?" Lars' voice was clinical, but worry crept in.

"Yeah, I couldn't catch my breath just now. I think it might have happened last night, too," she admitted. "And everything looks a little blurry."

"Her feet were much more swollen today than yesterday, as well," Fitz added, keeping his voice gentle.

Lars' sigh was agonized, followed by a pause on the other end of the line. "We can take your blood pressure to confirm, but, Belly, I think we know it's going to tell us you have preeclampsia, and it can progress very rapidly."

Clara went cold at his words, as if ice-water drenched her, and goosebumps rose all over her arms and neck.

"What does that mean?" Fitz asked, still steady but she could hear the underlying worry in his tone.

"It means that Clara's blood pressure has risen dangerously. It's critical she stay calm and get to a hospital with intensive care as quickly as possible. I'm a few hours away." Clara could hear the frustration in his voice, even though he masked it. "Don't wait for me, though. Just start driving to Colestown right away. You shouldn't stop to bring anything."

Clara knew from her reading after her OB had mentioned her slightly elevated blood pressure that preeclampsia was incredibly dangerous. It could come on suddenly and was life-threatening for mother and child. She took a wobbly breath and was grateful for the warm pressure of Fitz's hand closing around hers. *Steady. Solid.*

"When you get there, we may have to have her flown to Duluth or even the Twin Cities. Please let them know right away when you arrive, and I'll call them as soon as we disconnect. I'd have them fly to you now, but there was an accident on thirty-five with a big rig so you'll make better time driving at first." Lars' voice was calm—gentle—but Clara knew this was exactly what he'd feared—a complication with her in this remote area and the baby three weeks early on top of it all.

"Do you remember your promise, Lars?" Clara asked.

She thought she heard her brother's voice hitch on the other end of the line, but she couldn't be sure. "I do, Belly, but maybe we'd better tell Fitz as well." He made the statement a question.

"Yes," Clara agreed.

"Fitz, since you'll be there with her, if it comes down to a situation where only one of them can be saved, Clara wants to be certain that it is the baby instead of her. Understood?" Lars' voice was definitely heavy.

Fitz squeezed her hand, hard. "Understood," he answered in a thick voice. He cleared his throat before he spoke again, the intensity in his eyes as he looked at Clara obvious even through the blurriness. "Lars, if there was a way to get Clara to St. Paul Memorial in under an hour and have an OB surgeon standing by, that might make a difference, right?"

Lars' reply was instant. "Yes, depending on the situation, it could be a game-changer. Hopefully an unnecessary precaution, but certainly best. Unrealistic, though. You'd have to have a private jet. Do you have Navy or Air Force pilot friends stationed close by?" The hope in his voice was unmistakable. Clara wasn't sure what Fitz was referring to, either, but it sounded like it could really be important for her and the baby.

"Something like that. Could you call St. Paul Memorial and give the details to Dr. Noonan? Have him paged if you can't reach him. Tell him the request is from Colin Fitzhugh."

"How can you —?" she started to ask, but Fitz broke in before she could finish.

"Trust me, Clara?" There was a yearning in his voice she couldn't fail to respond to. A sadness. As if he needed and dreaded hearing that she trusted him.

She didn't even have to consider it. Whatever else he was, he was someone she believed in. Honorable and kind. "Yes, of course," she confirmed.

He let out a relieved breath. "I'll explain everything as we go. Lars, you good?"

"Sure, I'll call SPM right away," her brother answered. "Thank you... That's it, just *thank you*," he said, the breadth of his gratitude in his voice.

"Don't thank me yet. Thank me when you're visiting Clara and Baby O in the hospital, all right?"

"All right. Keep me posted," Lars answered.

"Will do." Fitz pressed the screen to end the call.

Before she could even react or ask the multitude of questions racing through her mind, first and foremost of which was how he planned to pull a private plane out of the thin air of Cameronville, Minnesota, Fitz had dialed again, obviously from memory. This time he held the phone to his ear so she couldn't hear. "Hi, Roger. Are you with my grandfather?"

She didn't know what she had expected, but Fitz sounded loving, affectionate. She heard a man's voice answer but couldn't hear the actual words. Curiosity about what Fitz was doing warred with worry over what was happening to her and the baby, and she took a deep breath to steady herself. Whatever it was, Fitz was trying to help her. *Was* helping her. That much was obvious. And it would have to be enough for now.

"I'm fine. Tell him I'm absolutely fine. I'm calling for..." He paused and looked over at Clara. "A very special friend. I'm sorry I don't have time to explain now, but we're in a hurry. Is the Cessna still at that little airport near Cameronville? And one of your pilots?"

The answer from the other end of the line was short. "Oh, thank *God*," Fitz breathed, his relief almost a tangible thing. "Can you call Mac and have him file a last-minute flight plan from Cameronville to MSP? And have the chopper waiting there to take us to St. Paul Memorial? They'll be expecting us, but could you make arrangements?"

Another short answer. Clara wished she knew what was being said, and who the heck Roger was.

"Thank you, Roger. Truly, thank you. I wouldn't trust anyone else." Fitz's words were thick with emotion. For her? She was distracted when he spoke again, obviously answering the other man.

"Yes, please do that. That's perfect. We'll see you soon." With those cryptic words, mysterious to her anyway, he disconnected the call.

"Okay, what the heck is going on?" Clara demanded.

Chapter Nine

The wariness in Clara's voice cut him like a razor. Mostly because she was right to be suspicious. He'd been lying to her. Or rather, not telling her the truth — but he didn't think she'd care much about that fine distinction at the moment. Frankly, even though he'd gone into combat missions he dreaded less than this conversation, it didn't matter. The situation boiled down to one reality. Clara, his beautiful, vibrant Clara, and her unborn child were in serious danger, and he was in a position to help them in a way that could save their lives.

When he thought of it that way, it didn't matter that he'd sworn never to use his family's influence again, that he'd walked away from it many years earlier and never looked back. It didn't even matter if he lost her trust. Hell, she could hate him after all was said and done. But as long as she was alive to hate him, he didn't care. That was all he wanted.

With a sick feeling in the pit of his stomach, which he very much feared was the death of the hopes and dreams he'd tried not to build around this woman but which had crept in all the same, he took a deep breath. "Oh-kay. So those Fitzhughs, the wealthy, powerful Twin Cities Fitzhughs of Fitzhugh Manufacturing? I'm one of them. The estranged, black sheep member of the family but, yeah." He tried to gauge her reaction, but she mostly looked surprised...and suddenly vulnerable.

"You can choose whether or not you believe me, honey, but I planned to tell you. Soon. Just not this way. I'll answer anything you want once we're on the plane. For now, we should get moving. That was my grandfather's butler who I called. He's really his right-hand man — been with him for forty plus years. Totally trustworthy. Roger'll make sure the private plane is ready for us when we get to the air field. I told my grandfather not to keep it there, that it wasn't necessary, but he's a wickedly stubborn old man who worries way too much about his grandson. And goddamn if I'm not unbelievably grateful for that now. He's even had a pilot staying in the area."

"I don't know how I feel," she answered, sticking out her stubborn chin. He'd known his feisty Clara wouldn't like this.

"Baby, you don't have to decide that now. You can take all the time in the world to decide how you feel as soon as you and your little one are stable."

"I hate that you didn't tell me. I do know that much," she said, temper creeping into her tone.

"Totally deserved. I was being self-indulgent, telling myself it was better for you but really wanting everything on my terms. It doesn't matter now. I just want you safe. Please let me do this for you, if for no other reason than because you helped me when I needed it." As the words left his mouth, he realized with sudden clarity that he wasn't doing this out of gratitude at all or to repay a debt. He was so worried, and so terrified, for this woman because he cared for her...deeply. He didn't want to look too closely at his feelings or name them, couldn't even believe he had them. After trying so hard to keep her at arm's-length, instead she'd crept right into his heart and made herself at home there.

No matter his feelings, he knew what he suggested made sense, and he trusted her to see that. And if she didn't, well, he wasn't above using other tactics. He would make sure she got on the plane and to the hospital, one way or another. The alternative was too awful to consider.

She considered his words for the briefest of times, then nodded. "Of course...*of course*." Her answer was hesitant at first, becoming firmer. "And thank you. I'll have to think about how I feel about us later, if there is an *us* at all," she gestured between them, and her comment hurt, physically hurt his chest, to see her uncertainty.

He'd done that. He deserved that.

"But if we make it through this, I'll always feel grateful for your help for me and my child," she finished.

Part of him just cracked and melted inside of his chest. She was so gracious, even when she was angry. He'd take it. Once she was safe, he could work on fixing things. It sounded like he might have a helluva lot of work, but he was up for it. She was worth it.

Not wanting to give her a chance to have second thoughts, he turned the key, gunned the engine and turned the truck around, heading back for the main roads. He'd paid attention to the route they'd taken from town, and he already knew how to get to the airport. His leg, head and even his wrist ached with how much he'd done, but he didn't care. He just set the pain aside, as he always did, and drove them straight to the airport.

Clara had driven by Cameronville Airport countless times growing up — well, airport was too grand a name for it, really — air field was more appropriate — an air field with a hangar. But she'd never paid that much attention to it. When they drove up now, she noticed every detail. There were a few small planes there, mostly looking older, some of them even dating from the Second World War. Then there was one gorgeous, gleaming marvel of modern aviation engineering that stood out like a sore thumb.

"That's our ride?" she asked, motioning toward the plane with her thumb. Her vision had cleared somewhat, so she could make out more of Fitz's facial expressions. Right then he looked pained, as if he almost didn't want to answer, to confirm that, yes, he had let her believe he was a humble soldier when really he had a freaking private jet at his disposal.

"One of my grandfather's toys, yes," he confirmed, sounding reluctant.

And what a toy it is, she thought. Her surprise only deepened when she saw a guy who looked like he'd stepped straight out of *Top Gun*, complete with a bomber jacket and reflective, aviator sunglasses and a cocky grin to match, come around the side of the plane.

"Who the heck is *that*?" she asked.

Fitz's frown only deepened, and he looked apologetic. "Joe MacKenzie. Mac. He's…not as much as an asshole as he looks. He's a former Navy pilot, and medic. He works for my grandfather full-time now. I can actually fly a Cessna, too, but…my reflexes aren't what they used to be."

She didn't know what to say.

"My grandfather has been a little…crazy about my health since I was in the hospital for so long. He wouldn't budge, insisting he wanted the Cessna and Mac here, at least for a while, and I couldn't stop him," Fitz explained.

When Clara realized what he was actually saying — that Joe MacKenzie was a pilot who his grandfather had apparently employed full-time to hang out in Cameronville and do nothing — her mind boggled at the extravagance, at the depth of wealth and privilege that Fitz's family must have to be able to do such a thing. She was startled from her thoughts by another sharp pain in her ribs that made her gasp. Gosh, it felt like she was being sliced right open.

All the worry for her baby and for her own health came rushing back in a flood. She was scared, truly terrified, that something might go wrong before they got help. Her breaths came more quickly, and she tried to fight off the panic that threatened, knowing it wouldn't do them any good. Could, in fact, make it worse.

Then suddenly Fitz was at her side — large, solid, reassuring. He opened her door, unclipped her from her seat belt, and lifted her right out of the truck in his huge, muscular arms. "Just breathe, honey. Let me take care of you. I'm going to carry you to the plane, and we'll get you to the hospital in no time," he murmured against her hair, and she held on to his voice and confidence like a lifeline. She vaguely felt him wince when he had her full weight, but he never betrayed any other sign of strain. He conveyed complete calm, as if he had no doubts that she'd be fine — that they'd all be fine.

Mac met them quickly, his voice only slightly winded from running. "I can take her," he offered.

"*No.*" Fitz's response was instant, and more of a growl than a word. "No," he repeated more reasonably, "I've got Clara. But if you could get the door open so I can lift her right up to you, I'd appreciate it."

"Yeah, sure, man. I didn't know how things were. Just trying to help." Mac's voice was apologetic, and Fitz grunted an acknowledgment.

"Is she in labor?" Mac asked.

"Preeclampsia, we think. Possibly severe," Fitz answered in a clipped tone, but Clara could hear the underlying emotion.

"Got it, okay," Mac replied, matching Fitz's calm tone. "We'll take care of you, Clara," he added before he ran back toward the plane. She noticed he ran with a slightly lopsided gait but was fast nonetheless.

Clara knew she ought to be concerned that she looked so bad that people were running to help her. And terror was a real thing, coiled cold in the pit of her stomach, but she also felt oddly protected...cherished. The way Fitz held her, as if she were the most precious thing in the world to him, and his total command, gave her the strength to keep the fear at bay. She concentrated on breathing as each step jarred her a little.

When they reached the plane, they stopped and Fitz's voice rumbled under her cheek. "I'm lifting you up to Mac now, baby, but I'll be right next to you again as soon as I climb up."

She nodded and felt herself airborne for an instant before a second set of muscular arms caught her and pulled her into the plane. Another pain hit, along with a wave of dizziness, and she breathed through it. When she looked around again, she saw that she was settled into a leather seat, reclined, and Mac was watching her with concern. She couldn't help but notice he was extremely handsome, with blond hair the color of butter, cut very short, a strong jaw and kind green eyes.

He kneeled and was opening a bag when Fitz joined them on the small plane as well. The tightness around Fitz's eyes and mouth were the only outward signs of strain, but his eyes blazed with purpose and determination. He held her gaze for a long moment, and she saw something in his expression that made her heart jump in her chest. But then he looked and away and went to crouch uncomfortably next to Mac.

She looked around then, too, finally noticing the interior of the plane. It wasn't spacious, but it was certainly luxurious, with pale leather seats that felt supple under her fingers, shining wooden inlays and what looked like a mini bar and kitchenette to one side.

The two men returned, Mac holding a mobile blood pressure monitor, and Fitz with a smaller, white bag that rattled slightly as he moved.

"Hi there, Clara. I'm Joe MacKenzie—Mac to my friends, which I hope you'll consider me." His grin was wide, white and very reassuring, and she thought that Lars would be impressed by his bedside manner. "I haven't been a medic for a little while now, but I was trained by the best in the US Navy and I've worked as an EMT as well. I'd like to take your blood pressure before we take off, just so we can give the hospital some more information, if that's all right?"

Fitz squeezed her hand with his rough one, and his face looked reassuring. "Of course," she said, but her voice sounded weaker than she'd expected. "I took it this morning and it was on the high side of normal — exact same it's been for a week straight."

He positioned the cuff on her arm and it did its thing, tightening and beeping, then loosening with aching slowness. When it finally released, the machine let out a series of high-pitched bleeps, which Mac cut off abruptly by pressing a button. The face he turned to her and Fitz was calm, but his eyes betrayed his worry.

"All right, so I'm going to level with you. Your blood pressure's really high right now. You're doing the right thing getting to the hospital as quickly as possible. I want you to turn to your left side as much as possible, and relax as much as you can. I'm going to give you a low dose of something that should help a little, but we can't give you much."

Clara's eyes filled with tears. "Is it dangerous for the baby?" she asked. Fitz's grip on her hand was solid and reassuring, anchoring her when she was suddenly feeling so adrift.

"Not this amount, no. It's safe. But because it's a low dose, it also might not help that much, so it'll be important that you stay as calm as you can. The only real cure for preeclampsia is childbirth, so I'm going to proceed as if that's the most likely next course of treatment." Mac's honesty made her trust him, even though she didn't like what he was saying.

"Mac and I will take good care of you, honey. The best. So you can lie back and just think about how happy you're gonna feel when you get to meet Baby O."

Clara turned to Fitz as he spoke, peering into his roughly handsome, beautiful face that she'd come to care about so much. Her vision had cleared again, for which she was grateful. Fitz's eyes were worried, but so achingly tender she almost had to look away. She believed him when he said she'd be safe. "Thank you," she whispered.

Fitz's expression was intent, but he tried to give her a reassuring smile. It failed, but she appreciated the effort. "Anything for you, baby," she thought he murmured, but couldn't be totally sure.

Mac gave her a quick injection and she got settled into the seat so that she lay reclined on her left side. Fitz rubbed her back gently, then stroked one finger down her cheek. The tenderness of the gestures warmed her and made some of her terror melt away. Without words, he reassured her. Impossibly, she must have fallen asleep because when she next opened her eyes, Fitz was lifting her from the plane to a stretcher.

Everything became a blur then, with other people around, Mac included, as they went out into the bright sunshine and onto another plane. A helicopter, this time. Someone—she wasn't sure who, but she looked like a nurse—hooked up leads and an EEG monitor to her as they walked, and a tight banded monitor around her stomach as well, for the baby. The roar of the rotors was nearly deafening as they got closer, blowing strong winds everywhere, but then she was on the helicopter, and she felt the unique weightlessness that meant they were in the air again. Through everything, the only constant was Fitz at her side—watching her and making sure she had everything she needed — making sure she knew he would take care of her.

It seemed they were landing again almost as soon as they took off this time, but of course, she knew the Minneapolis-St. Paul Airport wasn't very far from St. Paul Memorial Hospital. They landed on what looked to be the top of the building, and when they lowered her stretcher, they were met by an even larger group of people, all looking very urgent.

They talked over her as they ran.

"BP spiked to one-ninety over one-twenty but seems to have partially stabilized." That voice sounded like Mac's.

"Thanks," a voice near her head on her right side responded. "Jody, do we have confirmation on whether the OR is ready yet?"

"Room Seven is set up," an efficient voice confirmed near her feet.

They were inside now, in a long hallway that held the unique mix of antiseptic and disinfectants hospitals always seemed to smell like, and the stretcher came to a stop. The man near her head, who was distinguished-looking with streaks of white at his temples, leaned down to speak to her directly.

"Hi, Clara, I'm Dr. Noonan. I spoke with your brother, Dr. Olafson, earlier and we've got everything ready for your arrival."

He seemed nice, and his manner was kind and professional all at once. As the close relative of two doctors, she could appreciate that. But she wished Fitz were still there, too.

"Fitz?" she murmured his name before she realized what she'd done, and like magic, he was next to her, taking her softer hand into his rough one.

"Right here, honey. Dr. Noonan is an old friend, and a career OB surgeon. You'll be in the best of hands." His voice was gentle, but her mind seized on one word.

"Surgeon?"

Dr. Noonan's face appeared in her line of vision again. "I'm afraid so, Clara. Along with the severity of your other symptoms, your blood pressure is too high for us to wait at all, even for a spinal block or epidural, and the baby is healthy but showing some early signs of distress as well. With your permission, we'd like to go forward right away with a Caesarian section under general anesthesia."

It was silly. She didn't know why her face felt suddenly cool from tears that trailed in fat drops down her cheeks. "I wanted to deliver at home. No drugs. Nothing against them, but..." she trailed off.

"Baby, I'm so sorry," Fitz said, and she could hear real regret. It touched her that he understood, but he reminded her of what it meant to be strong.

She sighed. "Okay...okay." She took a shaky breath. "It really sounds like this surgery is what's best for both of us. Let's go ahead—and thank you."

"Good." Dr. Noonan nodded. "We'll get started right now, then," he said in a professional tone, "and you'll be holding your little one before you know it," he added kindly.

"Fitz—" she started, but the doctor cut her off, nicely but firmly.

"Will have to wait in the waiting room. We have full surgical and NICU teams in there already, but we'll come out with news as soon as we can."

With that, before she even had a chance to react, her hand was no longer in Fitz's and they were moving again, away from Fitz's solid, reassuring bulk and into a large, bright room, filled with people. It felt freezing. They gave her an injection as they put a mask on her, then everything faded to black.

Chapter Ten

Fitz had never liked waiting. It had been the worst part of most of his missions — the tension, the constant readiness, never knowing when or where or even *if* a threat would manifest. It was almost as grueling as the combat itself, but in a totally different way. The state of high alert had lasted and lasted until he'd almost cracked a couple of times from the sheer tension of it. Now, waiting to find out whether Clara and her baby were safe was pure agony.

He hadn't known if he'd be able to stand the hospital — had even worried the smells, the sounds, would give him flashbacks — but knowing *she* was here was enough to make him able to stay, to face just about anything. The minutes ticked by like hours as he perched on the edge of one of the molded-plastic waiting-room chairs. He stood, prowling the room, until he finally sat down again. When he checked his watch, only five more minutes had elapsed. He swore under his breath and was startled when someone answered.

"I'd tell you not to think about it, that what's going to happen will happen and she's getting the best care possible, but I don't think you'd listen...as usual."

"Shit, Mac, I didn't even hear you come in," Fitz said, turning to the man. They'd met in the military hospital near San Diego—the first one Fitz had been in—though Mac had been much closer to recovery. The Navy pilot had been an inspiration to Fitz, with his positive attitude, even in the face of the amputation of his right leg below the knee. To look at him now, one would never know one of his legs was partly prosthetic unless someone told them.

Mac was one of the few people Fitz had trusted with the secret of who his family was. When Mac had mentioned he was looking for a new start, away from the pine forests of Georgia where he'd grown up, Fitz had mentioned that his grandfather was often hiring trustworthy pilots. It was generally a slow, cushy job, where the primary requirements were patience and integrity, but it was as good a place as any to regroup and get paid for it. He'd heard Mac had gotten the job but he hadn't kept in too close touch with the man. He hadn't kept in close touch with anyone, really.

Mac held two cups of coffee from the local gourmet coffee chain. "One of these is for you, if you want it."

Fitz took one gratefully. "Thanks, man."

Mac shrugged. "I thought you could use it. I had to call your grandfather, then I asked at the nurse's station, but it sounded like it might be a bit longer."

When he had asked about Clara's condition a little while earlier before calling Lars to update him, Fitz had gotten the same impression. The procedure was ongoing. But no news was sometimes good news. At least it wasn't bad. He scrubbed his hand over his face.

"She must mean a lot to you. How in the hell did you ever find her, by the way? Last I heard, you were going to the woods to do some soul-searching."

Fitz laughed. "I wouldn't have called it that, but I was spending some time in the state forest right near her cabin when I lost my footing and took a bad fall. She saved me, actually. Marched right in, picked me up and helped me. *Fearless*. I haven't known her that long but yeah, she means a lot to me."

"Unsolicited word of advice, then, from someone who knows what…well, just someone who knows." Mac's eyes had gone dark. "Don't make her keep guessing. When you're lucky enough to somehow, in this vast world, find a truly wonderful woman, do anything you have to do so she understands how much she means to you."

Fitz raised his eyebrows. "Unsolicited is right. Right now, I'm just praying she's all right. If she is, I'm still going to have a lot of ground to make up with her."

Mac opened his mouth to say more, but whatever it was got lost as Dr. Noonan came into the room. Fitz looked at the older man, his heart suddenly feeling as though it were lodged in his throat and his knees threatening to give out.

"Clara and the baby made it through surgery fine, and she's already beginning to stabilize. She should be starting to come around in about fifteen minutes or so."

Gratitude was too tame a word for what he felt, hearing those words. Relief swept through him in such an intense wave he was just happy he hadn't dropped his coffee to the floor. "Thank God, oh, *thank God*," he said, feeling his eyes prickle suspiciously.

"Nice work, Doc," Mac added, and the older man smiled.

"Glad I could help," he answered, turning to Fitz. "I might have been called in on a case like this anyway, but Colin and I go way back. I knew his parents, in fact. Anytime, Colin, you just call me."

Mac looked curious, but he didn't comment, and the doctor began to leave. Fitz was more than happy to let the moment pass. Charles Noonan had been, and still was, a good man who'd had the misfortune to get caught up in the stormy affairs of Fitz's parents.

"Charles, is the baby a boy or girl?" Fitz called, when it hit him that they didn't know.

Dr. Charles Noonan turned back as a smile spread across his tired face. "Ah, yes, a little girl, with a thatch of reddish hair to match her mother's. They've taken her to the NICU, but it's mostly a precaution for observation. She's over seven pounds, with a good set of lungs."

"A girl," Fitz said wonderingly. He pictured a miniature version of Clara—outspoken, kind, funny. He sat down heavily on the unyielding molded-plastic chair again. Good Lord, the world was never going to be the same.

* * * *

Her eyes didn't want to open just yet, and her mind felt full of a swirling fog, but Clara knew there was something incredibly important. *Beep, whir, beep*. The sounds echoed around her. Quiet but so very noisy. One clear thought managed to pierce her consciousness and she opened her eyes with a snap.

"My baby?" she croaked.

"Your baby girl is healthy and doing well. I got to stop by the NICU to see her very briefly. They're just keeping her for observation, but the pediatrician said they'll bring her to meet you really soon."

The tension that had filled her body and gnawed at her stomach relented a little at Fitz's rough voice. "You're here," she said, realizing as the words left her mouth that they sounded idiotic. Obviously he was there, right in the room with her.

"Did you think you could get rid of me, honey? I wouldn't want to be anywhere else," he answered in a tone that was gruff and warm all at once, like the man himself.

She sniffed and felt tears leaking out of the corners of her eyes.

"Baby, baby," he said, his voice getting closer. "Don't cry. You're breaking my heart."

"I don't know why I'm crying. I'm so relieved I'm still alive. And oh my God, I have a daughter who's healthy. Then you're here, being so sweet. I'm just…it's like all of the gratitude and joy I'm feeling condensed like moisture in a raincloud and now it's time for a thunderstorm."

The chair that Fitz had pulled next to the bed dragged along the floor, making a prolonged low squeak. He lowered himself with a wince and took her left hand into both of his, warm against her cold skin. "That's all right, then. Raining joy is definitely allowed, although warn me if there's going to be lightning." His eyes crinkled at the corners, and he looked amused — weary, but happy and just as devastatingly handsome as she remembered.

She knew she couldn't possibly look good. Not that it mattered — she'd just had major, emergency surgery, for heaven's sake. But something about Fitz's expression made her feel incredibly beautiful, amazing and powerful. Something blazed behind his blue eyes, a mix between admiration, awe and something deeper. It made her breath catch in the back of her throat.

There was a sound at the door before she could say anything, then a tall, well-rounded woman in scrubs was there, wheeling a clear, plastic cart in front of her that looked like some sort of mini-incubator. Her smile was kind and genuine. "Oh, good, you're awake. We just now got approval from the NICU to release this little lady, so I wanted to bring her right to you."

With a sense of the surreal, Clara saw a tiny movement in the little bed. Her eyes went wide.

"Mama, here's your daughter," the nurse continued, gathering up the little, swaddled form, and approaching the bed with the baby in her arms.

Clara drank in every detail of the little red face—the chubby cheeks, crinkled eyes, sweet little nose and lips, stubborn chin. To her delight, she saw that her daughter's hair, which there was a lot of, was dark but with a distinct reddish tint. "She's gorgeous," she breathed, and the little eyes cracked open.

Love filled her, instant, intense and complete, pouring into and through her. She'd known she cared about her baby when she was carrying her. But this—meeting her—was something totally different. She looked up at Fitz and saw an expression of wonder on his face as well. His gaze was riveted to the baby.

"Is it...? Can I hold her?" she asked.

The nurse nodded, beaming. "We'll have to arrange you a bit, since you might not have a lot of strength in your arms right now, but absolutely. I think she'd love that."

Clara felt a thrill of excitement. *I'm going to hold my baby.*

"Dad, can you help me by placing pillows around her?" the nurse continued.

Fitz looked around in confusion at first, then understanding dawned on him. "Oh, uh, I'm not the dad," he said.

The nurse continued to smile. "Oops, sorry. You could have fooled me. Well, I hope you'll still help," she joked. Clara couldn't help but smile as well at her matter-of-fact attitude.

"Of course," Fitz answered, standing and arranging the multitude of pillows all around her.

Then suddenly her baby was in her arms. The little girl was light, but she still felt heavier than Clara expected, and her daughter's face looked rounded and healthy. "Hello, sweetheart," Clara whispered, and her vision blurred again with tears as the baby's eyes opened again and she yawned, opening her mouth and making a distinct "*aaah*" sound. "I'm your mama, and I'm so happy to meet you. I want you to know that you are loved." Clara spoke to her daughter, stroking a finger over her soft little cheek.

Fitz coughed and sounded gruff, while the nurse just beamed.

Studying the little face, Clara knew without a doubt what she would call her daughter. She was glad she'd waited to decide.

"I'm going to name her Hope," she announced.

"Honey, that's a beautiful name," Fitz answered, his voice sounding more hoarse than usual. "I think it suits her perfectly." Then he spoke to the baby, holding his finger out to her where she had managed to wangle one hand out of the swaddling. "Pleased to meet you,

Hope. You have a wonderful mama." The baby grabbed his finger, making it look huge in her tiny hand, and held firm.

A bark of laughter escaped him, and he looked up into Clara's face, his eyes lit with surprise and delight. "She's so strong, Clara Belle."

A warm glow washed over Clara. They might have taken a bumpy road to get here, and she didn't know where the road was leading from here, either, but this moment—this one moment in time—was perfect. She'd survived pain and danger to be here, and now she held her daughter in her arms and had the man she was coming to care for very deeply at her side. It was much more than enough.

* * * *

The next few days passed in a blur of exhaustion, medicine and learning all about infant care. The nurse, whose name was Ellen, told Clara that she and another nurse named Kirsten would be her dedicated team, available any time day or night only for her or Hope. She hadn't known that hospitals did anything like that, but she supposed in such a state-of-the-art facility, they were certain to have best practices. There were other nurses, too, and doctors, who all showed them how best to change diapers, give baths, swaddle tightly and feed baby Hope. Fitz stayed by her side through all of it, sleeping on the uncomfortable pull-out chair every night, even though it must have felt terrible. He held and cuddled the baby often, giving her occasional bottles as well, and was quick to press the button to call the nurses at the slightest sign of overtiredness or pain from Clara, which she complained about but secretly found ridiculously endearing.

Lars visited as well, several times over the first two days. He was entirely enamored of his baby niece, totally losing his professional cool when he held her for the first time as he'd exclaimed over her "*perfect little fingers and toes.*" Clara planned to tease him relentlessly about that soon, but she'd wait at least a little while. Plus, he was right. Hope did have particularly adorable appendages. Then he'd gotten a call about another urgent situation back near Cameronville, and she'd urged him to return. It was nearly impossible for him to be away for more than a couple of days, ever. It had been the same for their father, so she understood. He'd looked reluctant but had finally agreed. Clara thought that Fitz must have said something to him as well, which made him feel more comfortable leaving her.

Mac had also visited several times, to her surprise. First, he'd brought a truly exquisite arrangement of white roses, lilies and chrysanthemums. Next, surprising her even more, he'd stopped by with an adorable blanket set and several onesies that fit Hope perfectly. When she hadn't hidden her surprise, he'd confessed that he was the proud uncle to several nieces and a nephew. She was dying to know more about him and his apparent friendship with Fitz, but she was too darn busy to ask.

She'd video-chatted with Amber as well, using their cell phones. Amber had loved seeing Hope, declaring that she and Bea would be best friends, despite their age difference. She was good for Clara's ego, too, telling her she looked radiant. There had been one awkward moment, though, when she'd asked about Clara's plans. Her original intent, of course, had been to return to the cabin for a while to settle in to motherhood, so she supposed that was still what would happen. Fitz had been acting like he might want to be a part of their future, but he hadn't said anything, so...she wasn't exactly sure what to think. Or why it left her feeling vaguely empty now to picture a life, even with baby Hope, that didn't include him.

The one other piece of information that had shadowed their days was the news that Mac had arranged for her bloodwork to be sent for special analysis, and he'd also had her home blood pressure monitor analyzed. The monitor had been broken — which was why she'd gotten such incorrect readings when she should have had early warning signs. More puzzling, though, was that she had no aspirin in her system at all. When he'd tried to find her bottle of baby aspirin, it had disappeared. She was certain she'd probably just dropped it someplace weird and that she'd find it as soon as she was back there, but the news was still unsettling.

On the night before the day they'd told her she would be released, after Kirsten, who was Ellen's counterpart overnight, had taken Hope to the nursery, Fitz had broached the subject of the future. Lying in the hospital bed, exhausted and groggy from the latest dose of medicine for the surgical pain, Clara was almost asleep before he started speaking.

"Clara," his voice rumbled in the dark.

"Mm-hm?" she answered, struggling to keep her eyes open.

"I meant to tell you earlier — so sorry, honey — but I've just been so darn tired. I made all the arrangements for you tomorrow."

Suddenly alert, Clara felt her chest tighten with apprehension. Was this goodbye, then? Just like that? "Oh?" she asked. Her question sounded small in the quiet room.

"I thought...well, hoped, really...that you and Hope might come to stay with me at my grandfather's for a while, so we could keep taking care of Hope together while you recover. And we have great security at the, uh, estate too."

Her heart had soared at his first statement, then dropped back down to a more pragmatic state as he finished. It made sense. It was very kind, too. He wanted to take care of her while she was still getting stronger. Getting over major surgery was no joke, and she knew that it would be just as difficult when she left the hospital — more difficult, for sure, if she were alone. She would be a fool not to agree. And if a little voice inside her head whispered that she'd wished for something more, especially after the way he'd acted as they'd traveled and right after she woke up from surgery, she ignored it.

"Thank you, Fitz. That's so generous of you and your grandfather. You've been just amazing," she said, keeping her voice friendly and polite, trying to match his tone.

"It's nothing. I would..." Was that disappointment she heard, or just her imagination? She anxiously awaited his next words. "I'm so happy I'm able to help," he finished lamely.

With that, the hope that had sprung up again was flattened. "Thank you again, and good night, Fitz," she said into the thick blackness of the room.

"Good night," he answered.

Despite how tired she was, she lay awake for a surprisingly long time before she slept.

Fitz called himself all kinds of a fool in his head as he lay on the uncomfortable chair that he'd slept on for the last three nights. 'Chair' was too kind a word for it. 'Wannabe Medieval Torture Device' would be a better name — or more accurate, at least. He'd had a chance to tell Clara what he was really feeling — that he wouldn't want to be anywhere but by her side, caring for her and Hope, that he'd broken the promise he'd made to himself years ago to never again rely on his family for anything to ensure that she had the best care, including private nurses, and that he was totally fine with that because she had come to mean that much to him, that he was so sorry that he'd lied and prayed that she could forgive him. But had he said any of those things? *No.* He'd let her think he was just being nice.

When the hell did I become such a coward? As he listened to her breathing slow and knew she'd finally fallen asleep, he took a long, hard look at his emotions. He knew he had trouble with trust. It was why he kept even some of his closest friends from knowing all of him by not telling them the truth of his past. Probably why, at least on an unconscious level, he'd kept it from Clara too. He hadn't wanted to see her reaction to his family, good or bad, and not to him.

He'd lived his youth in the shadow of the parent he'd looked so much like as to be uncanny — his father, Albert Olafson. *Bertie.* Bertie had been handsome, charismatic, smart and immensely wealthy. He'd had the world at his very fingertips, with a gorgeous wife who loved him, children who loved spending time with him and parents who trusted him and gave him anything and everything he'd asked for. But his charisma had hidden an inner selfishness and weakness, and the stunning picture their lives had made had been just that—a picture.

Bertie had slowly destroyed their family, making it crumble from the inside out. He'd openly been with other women, leaving his wife and children more and more frequently to spend time with mistresses. And money? He'd spent fortunes on his latest paramours when he hadn't taken care of his own children.

Oh, Fitz wasn't absolving his mother in this. She was certainly to blame as well, but she'd never been strong or courageous. As a noted society beauty, she'd conveyed the impression of pride, polish and utter loveliness. But Sabrina Cardell Fitzhugh had been hiding the truth behind a carefully constructed façade. She'd been so spoiled by her family and also by her husband, at first, that she was incapable or unwilling to take charge in anything, except for keeping up appearances. At that, she excelled so well that even Fitz's grandfather hadn't had any idea of the degree of the problems until Fitz's parents had died. She'd grown bitter and cruel over the years, as if nothing else mattered to her but that no one ever find out the truth behind the pretty picture.

A tragic accident, the press reported, but the truth was much uglier. His mother had insisted that they go to some particular party. His father had refused. A typical screaming match had ensued. The only difference was that his mother had apparently won, for a change, and they'd left, his father downing glasses of the Scotch he favored like water as they'd walked out of the door. He'd been driving too fast, and it had started to snow. The coroner said—privately to the family only, of course — that they'd had no chance at all when their car had hit an icy patch near one of the scenic lakes. They'd both died instantly before they could drown.

So, when someone told Fitz, as they frequently did, that he looked just like his father, was *just like* his father, even when they meant it as a compliment, it stung. The day he'd looked in the mirror and seen a man who not only looked like his father but had also started acting like him — that was the day he'd joined the Marine Corps. His brother and sister pretended that they loved and honored the hallowed memory of their wonderful, perfect parents, but Fitz couldn't. He just *couldn't*.

Fitz shifted in the chair, trying in vain to find a more comfortable position. He should have known it wasn't possible. He stilled at the loud creak that rang out in the room, hoping he wouldn't wake Clara. But her breathing remained slow and even. He was still so grateful to hear it, when he'd feared for her life.

He might not be worthy of her — in fact, he was sure of it — but that hadn't stopped his feelings. He didn't know if he could walk away now, but he knew without a doubt that he didn't want to. He vowed to try to show her, if he couldn't quite manage to tell her, how much he cared for her. He would be honest from here on out, letting her see him, his family, good, bad and ugly, since he wasn't sure at all how his siblings would react to his return. Then she could choose, and he would live with her choice. Hope flared, like a warmth deep in his gut, that she might see the truth of him and still choose him. With that, he closed his eyes and finally slept.

Chapter Eleven

Clara wasn't sure what she'd pictured when Fitz had said they'd be going to his grandfather's house, but the sprawling estate, complete with its own road and high security fences certainly wasn't it. A movement in the trees made her think there might even be guards around the perimeter. She should have known the family seat of the Fitzhughs would be massive. Sure, she'd thought it would be spacious, but this level of opulence was somewhat beyond her comprehension.

Fitz had insisted on a private ambulance for her and Hope, so the quick drive from St. Paul Memorial Hospital was made in total comfort. As Ellen had been settling them in, she finally realized the truth as she looked at the other mothers who were leaving the hospital at the same time. She'd been getting special treatment, with the private room and the dedicated nursing care. She wasn't sure how she felt about Fitz's not telling her.

The way she was positioned in the back of the ambulance, so that she had an unobstructed sight line right through the front windshield, also meant that she had a prime view of the mansion, rising tall and imposing from the hill at the end of a tree-lined drive. The architecture had touches of the Renaissance, with tall spires and turrets, and a stone exterior, like a European palace.

She was surprised when they didn't continue on to the main house, instead taking a smaller road that snaked to the left. At the end of it, she could see a much smaller house. Of course, anything would look small after the castle she'd just seen, and looking again, she guessed it was probably three stories tall, well-maintained and had a Victorian flair. In contrast to the grandeur of the main house, this one was much cozier...more homey.

"This is where we'll be staying," Fitz confirmed, and she could feel him watching her face closely. He'd probably seen her reaction to the behemoth of a family seat earlier too.

Something in her eyes must have prompted him to continue. "It's actually the original house my grandparents bought. Later, they bought more and more of the surrounding land and built the main house. 'Fitzhugh's Folly', the press calls it sometimes. Still, my grandparents never wanted to tear down or sell the original house, and they renovated it a few years ago and use it as a guest house. My grandfather's always saying he's going to move back out here, but it's easier for everyone with him in the main house."

"It's beautiful," she said, meaning the words. "The main house is" — she searched for a word that wouldn't offend, and settled on — "impressive." Fitz's chuckle told her he understood what she wasn't saying. "But this house is softer. It's large, but it still looks like a home."

Fitz looked pleased by her words. "I've always preferred it, myself. The Folly is such a showplace. It certainly impresses people, but it also intimidates, as it's meant to, I think. I don't want you to feel that way."

They rolled to a quiet stop in front of the large porch, complete with a porch swing. Hope had slept throughout most of the ride, with Clara's hand resting lightly on her, but she woke up with a squawk.

"Shhh…" Clara murmured. "It's all right, sweetie. We're here, and I'm sure we'll have you fed and settled in no time." She looked at Fitz questioningly as she spoke, hoping it was true.

He nodded. "Yes, I just came by this morning to double-check when you were having all those final tests. We've got you and Hope set up in adjoining rooms, with a crib and an infant travel crib, so you can use whichever you'd prefer. There's a full nursery set up, too, with diapers, bottles, clothes, changing table — everything the night nurse thought you might need."

"Fitz, that's amazing! I can't believe you did all of this…" She trailed off as she realized what he'd said. "What night nurse?"

Fitz looked sheepish. "Sorry, honey. I must have forgotten to mention her. I asked Lars to tell me what I could do to make you comfortable, and he said that a night nurse would make a big difference to you, recovering from emergency surgery. Her name is Judith, and she's been a private nurse for over ten years. I think — hope — you'll like her."

Clara's surprise and pleasure at his incredible thoughtfulness was genuine, but the uncomfortable sensation that felt suspiciously like shame prickled at her. Maybe 'shame' was too strong a word, but it didn't feel good. "I...don't know what to say." She, who always had an opinion, was surprised that it was true.

Fitz frowned. "I hope you'll like it."

She hated seeing his disappointment, so she rushed to reassure him. "I'm sure I will. It sounds spectacular. I just...really wish you'd mentioned it sooner. Or, maybe asked me?"

If Fitz responded, she didn't hear it over Hope's sudden wailing. He unclipped her carrier from the base, and a woman took it from him as the doors opened. Fitz helped Clara step down as well, holding her against his side as if she were made of glass. They passed through a grand entryway, complete with a stunning crystal chandelier, but she barely noticed it. Their rooms were up one short flight of stairs, which Fitz helped her take slowly, and finally they entered a room that was clearly a nursery.

Hope was quieting down as the woman finished changing her tiny diaper on a pristine wicker changing table that wouldn't have been out of place in baby design magazine, if such a thing existed. Again, it was beautiful. The woman, who was obviously there to help with Hope and seemed very capable, was friendly as she introduced herself. But that same uncomfortable sensation still nagged at Clara. It made her feel irritable and out of sorts.

Fitz guided her to the large glider, complete with a gliding footstool, which was placed near the crib. She sat down gratefully, and the twinge of pain reminded her that she needed to take more medicine soon...after she fed Hope.

Fitz handed the baby to her, and Hope settled down almost immediately as Clara began to nurse her. It calmed both of them, really. Clara put her feet up and leaned back, and it felt lovely. She realized that, while she wasn't entirely comfortable with the arrangements, it certainly made things easier. Way easier, in fact. After being raised with all of this around him, what in the world had made Fitz leave it for the difficulties and very real danger of the Marine Corps? She vowed to ask him as soon as she had the chance.

Everyone left her and Hope alone while the baby ate, which Clara appreciated. As soon as Hope drifted off to sleep, she rose and put her in the center of the enormous crib mattress, its size emphasizing just how tiny the baby was. Clara marveled at the level of detail that had gone into decorating the room, from the little yellow duckies on the crib sheet and tasteful mobile, to the eyelet lace curtains and framed paintings of animals. It was fresh, clean and very peaceful. She sat back down on the glider with a wince, deciding to rest for just a moment more before she went in search of her medicine.

She must have fallen asleep because soft voices outside of her room woke her up. Not wanting them to wake the baby, though that seemed unlikely with how soundly Hope seemed to sleep, she stood and crossed the room to the door, intent on closing it.

"...don't want your good nature to be taken advantage of by a scheming gold-digger." She didn't recognize the voice, but she froze in place at the words.

"Stay out of this, Drew. I don't need, nor do I want, your interference. What I choose to do is none of your damn business." The second voice was Fitz's, and he sounded coldly angry.

"You've forgotten what it's like to be a Fitzhugh, brother, with women constantly throwing themselves at you, each of them hoping you'll buy her beautiful things, or even better, that she'll be the one to make you settle down and she'll have everything she wants for the rest of her life." The similarity of the voice to Fitz's, along with his words, made it obvious that this man must be his brother, but the bitterness in his voice, the world-weary quality, was very different.

"I don't need to defend her to you, but I'm going to. You couldn't be more off base on this, Drew. Clara isn't like that. And I'm sorry that something must have happened in your past to make it so easy for you to believe that about women." Clara was warmed by Fitz's defense of her, and she'd also heard the sympathy in his voice for his brother.

"It's a belief that is well-founded and hard-earned." The sadness this time was unmistakable, and Clara couldn't help but feel an answering compassion for the unknown Drew as well as she started to pull the door shut, only to freeze again at his next words. "I'm sorry, Colin, but one of Lana's friends knows her from the law firm where she worked, and he confirmed that she targets wealthy men."

Clara waited, her hand still on the doorknob, and waited to hear Fitz's response. Instead, his long silence was deafening. At last, he spoke. "Who is that? What's his name?" he asked.

Anger and righteous indignation flashed through her, white-hot, at his reasonable tone. She couldn't believe that Fitz, who she'd trusted with her pain of how her relationship with Brock had ended, was ready to just believe something like that of her. Oh, sure, he hadn't actually said that, but he didn't seem too upset, either, just asking for more information. Her anger rose until she was practically shaking, but behind it, and much worse, was the sadness and the deep feeling of betrayal. *What am I doing here, anyway?* She hadn't asked for any of this. In fact, she was deeply uncomfortable with all her surroundings. This wasn't her lifestyle, and clearly, she wasn't up for playing with the bigwigs. She always just seemed to get burned.

With that righteous thought, she pushed the door open in a huff, startling the two men who both turned to look at her. Fitz's brother, Drew, looked surprised and a little wary, although he hid it well, like a good poker player. Or, she thought, like the good businessman that he apparently was. Fitz tried to hide it but he looked angry. Furious, in fact. Well, she didn't care if he chose to believe a lie, and it made him mad.

"Hi, pleased to meet you, Drew, is it?" She pasted her best Minnesota Nice smile on her face, the one that Lars told her made her look like a shark. "I'm Clara, the scheming gold-digger who targets wealthy men. Oh, but you already know that, don't you? My infant daughter and I will be leaving as soon as she wakes up and I can make arrangements with someone who doesn't believe that I'm a shallow, wannabe trophy wife. It's phenomenal how I knew that I would just stumble over my next rich target lying on the ground in the woods, isn't it?" She knew she was raising her voice, but she was good and mad...and hurt.

She leveled a glare at Fitz, who was looking stunned, then confused. "I thought better of you. A lot better." She finished speaking on a whisper, and turned on her heel to go, but her exit was spoiled by a wince, and she stumbled a bit when her vision had gone suddenly wobbly from unshed tears.

Fitz wasn't sure who he was more upset with—his brother, for coming over self-righteously, under the guise of being helpful after they'd hardly spoken for several years, or himself for acting like a man who Clara could believe, even for a moment, thought that she was some sort of gold-digger based on the weak authority of one of his sister Lana's friends.

He glowered at Drew, who took a step back. His brother was visibly surprised, and understanding was apparently dawning on him that he'd been wrong...very wrong. "I'm not finished with this conversation, but I'm going to talk to Clara first, and hopefully I can somehow convince her to stay."

Drew nodded. He wasn't the kind of man to apologize, so he didn't, but his blue eyes, so similar to Fitz's own, were clearly filled with regret.

Fitz didn't knock at Clara's door, not wanting to give her the chance to refuse him entry. She was sitting on the brass daybed he'd thought, just that morning, suited her so perfectly. It was old-fashioned but lovely, covered with one of the quilts his grandmother had made by hand, and reminded him forcibly of the bed Clara had given him at the cabin. She had her phone in her hand and was looking at it.

He knew she must have heard him come in—he wasn't as stealthy as he'd once been, with his limp—but she didn't look up. He chose to take that as a good sign and crossed the room to sit next to her on the bed. When he saw the silvery trail of one tear snaking down her pink cheek, he nearly growled with anger.

"Honey," he said gently, putting his hand on her back. "Please don't leave. It's the last thing I want. I don't believe for one second that you would take advantage of me or any other man for his money."

The sad face she turned toward him, so flushed and upset, was like a punch to the gut...with brass knuckles.

"Why didn't you deny it to your brother?" she asked in a small voice.

He took her hands into his. "You didn't give me long enough to finish. I wanted the name of whoever told such an outright lie about you so that I could find him. But, baby, anyone who knows you would know it's an absurd accusation."

She looked away from him and he saw two more tears run down her cheeks.

"Damn, did I say something wrong again? I'm trying but...sometimes I can be a little rough. I blame the years in the Corps." Fitz racked his brain for what he'd said wrong, but he was mystified. He hated that he'd caused Clara pain.

She shook her head. "No, it's not you. I just...a lot of people believed that of me, *before*. I told you about Brock, but I didn't tell you that most of my coworkers sided with him. You know, the smooth, charming partner was much better liked than the overreaching paralegal. My last month there, there were only about three people who didn't give me the cold shoulder. Luckily, one of the other partners, the one who had initially hired me, was one of them or I wouldn't have had any of the contract work."

Fitz tucked a strand of her bright, fuzzy hair behind one of her ears and hated all her former coworkers and colleagues who'd made her feel that way, who'd been willing to believe the worst of her after knowing her. "I'm so sorry, baby."

Her lips curved into a small smile, but it was forced. "I appreciate that. And I guess I'm just a little...oversensitive about those types of accusations. I shouldn't have reacted the way I did."

Relief and hope rose within him, only to sink back down again as she continued.

"But I still can't stay here. *We* can't stay here."

"Why?" he asked simply.

She gestured around the room. "Look at this. *All* of this. We don't belong on an estate in a designer nursery-bedroom suite with a night nurse. This bedspread alone probably costs as much as every ratty old garment I wore at the cabin with you combined. I learned, the very hard way, that this world isn't for me."

Behind her words, Fitz heard the old hurt, and also panic. He took a deep breath and tried a different tack. His Clara was passionate but pragmatic, too. It was one of the things he liked best about her.

"It's overwhelming. I understand. Hell, I grew up with it, but I'm still surprised every time I have to come back. I left to escape it, and maybe that's what we want to do again. But baby, give me a chance?" He took a deep breath and tried not to beg, even though he would, if that's what it took. "You told me you trusted me. I know I wasn't entirely truthful, because I was so used to keeping this secret, but I hope you still trust me at least a little bit. Won't you please stay until you're more recovered, and Hope isn't so much of a newborn? You can even view it as fair payment for saving my life, if that makes you stay. Hope won't have to move, and she'll have the best possible care while you get back to one hundred percent. Eight weeks, then you can leave without looking back. Will you do that?"

His heart was in his throat as he watched her think about it. Finally, she nodded, and he let out a breath he hadn't realized he'd held.

"Thank you, honey." Even as he answered, the plan came together in his mind. He'd messed things up, big time, keeping the secret of his background, but now he'd bought himself eight weeks. He would use the time to convince her, in every way that he could think of, that he was a good partner for her and father for Hope. With crystal clarity, he saw that they were what he'd been searching for, and he wanted them in his life. Forever.

Clara was about to learn first-hand how tenacious and determined a Marine could be

Chapter Twelve

Clara's cheeks and stomach hurt from laughing so much at Fitz, who was currently doing a credible, full-body gorilla impression, to Hope's apparent delight. The baby didn't smile, of course, but her liquid blue eyes were huge, following his every movement, and her darling cupid's bow lips twitched. After six weeks, Clara couldn't remember being so happy...ever.

From the very first night at the house, Fitz had insisted on splitting feedings with her so that, with the help of the night nurse, she was able to get enough rest to feel much better relatively quickly. Clara had read, and heard, so many stories of new mothers, even ones who'd had normal deliveries, just running themselves into the ground. She hadn't experienced any of that and was so incredibly grateful to Fitz, who'd insisted she take care of herself as well as they took care of Hope. She might not spend twenty-four hours a day with her baby, but she got to spend every moment Hope was awake with her, enjoying every coo and gurgle—and she was convinced that Hope had the cutest little drool bubbles in creation — and she wasn't too exhausted and strung out to notice everything. Having meals cooked by the chef at the main house and sent over to them in batches had been a godsend as well. She would never have imagined she could get comfortable with such incredible luxury, and she still didn't feel entirely all right with it, but Fitz reminded her regularly that it was the least his family could do to thank her for taking care of him.

Now, with all the extra TLC and excellent meals, she had the energy to do even more, like walking around the grounds of the estate with little Hope in her stroller. Often, they visited the main house, where Fitz's grandfather, who insisted that she call him Pat, was delighted to see the baby. Roger tried to pretend he didn't like them, but it was all an act, and he was just as much of a softie as Pat was.

When Fitz had first taken her to meet his grandfather, about two weeks after they'd arrived, she'd found his brusque manner off-putting. He'd sat, a bent figure in a massive, velvet chair, waited on by the faithful Roger, clearly the master of his own little corner of the world. But the pleasure on his face when he'd seen Fitz had been very real, as well as the affection, so she'd given him the benefit of the doubt. When Fitz had had to leave the room with Roger, on some errand that she'd quickly realized had been made up to get her alone, Pat had grilled her relentlessly about her past, firing questions at her about everything from her family to what she'd written her undergraduate thesis on and corporate law. He'd finally sat back, satisfied, and practically cackled with glee.

When Fitz and Roger had returned, Pat had pronounced Clara a *"corker"*, and invited her to come visit any time with her *"wee nipper"*. She'd taken him at his word, and they'd both been satisfied with the visits, which were a lot of fun for everyone, including Hope, who seemed to like to grab and hold on to his very distinguished nose.

Fitz had told her he'd also come to an uneasy truce with Drew, who wasn't the total ass he'd remembered or that he'd seemed to be when she'd first met him. She'd met Fitz's sister, Lana, as well. She'd actually been quite young when Fitz had left, only sixteen and apparently flighty. Meeting the elegant and poised young woman Lana had become, Clara had a hard time reconciling his description of her with the reality. Fitz obviously had a lot of catching up to do with everyone.

Her very favorite times, though, were when the three of them — Fitz, Hope and she — were at home in the Victorian house. He was funny, silly and patient with Hope, and he flirted outrageously with Clara. He often brushed against her or touched her when he didn't need to. It made all her nerve endings sizzle, and she felt sexy, in spite of being the mother of a newborn.

This afternoon, it was rainy and blustery outside, so they'd set up the little baby blanket on the floor, with Hope's dangling toys above her. She seemed fascinated by the little jungle toys when she was on her back, but she'd let out a mighty wail of protest when Clara had flipped her onto her stomach for tummy time, and that was when Fitz had stepped in with his gorilla impression.

"I can't tell if she thinks I'm funny, believes I'm a gorilla or is just too stunned by me being a lunatic to look away," Fitz joked, grinning so that his dimple appeared in his cheek.

Clara glanced at Hope's rapt expression, then up at Fitz with a laugh. "I'd say odds are fifty-fifty gorilla vs. lunatic…but one hundred percent funny."

He gave an exaggerated wince. "Ouch. You wound me, Clara Belle. You Olafsons are a tough crowd."

As if to punctuate his statement, Hope cried again now that he'd stopped moving. In a move that had become almost as familiar to him as it was to Clara, Fitz bent and scooped Hope up, laying her gently on his shoulder.

"Getting too boring, little lady?" he asked. Clara smiled at him again when he caught her eye over Hope's bright head of hair.

"I think she's probably hungry…again." Clara sat down, arranging everything so she'd be ready to feed the baby.

"Is that right, bossy-pants? Are you hungry?" Fitz asked in a teasing voice, holding Hope up in the air gently before handing her to Clara. When Hope was feeding contentedly, he came around to sit on the couch next to them.

"Can I ask you something, Fitz?" she ventured.

He stilled next to her, obviously surprised, since she hadn't really initiated much serious conversation between them recently. "Anything, Clara. I don't want any secrets between us again…ever." His words were earnest, and he held her gaze as he spoke.

Clara wasn't sure she was ready to address a statement like that, but she sure as heck wasn't going to miss this chance. "Why did you choose the Marine Corps? I know you felt you had something to prove, and you wanted to get away from your family but...it must have been quite a difference."

It clearly wasn't the question he was expecting. "Fair question," he answered slowly, and thought for a moment before he continued. "I felt strongly — still feel — that it's a noble thing to protect and serve our country. I always heard stories about my Uncle Sean, a Marine, who fought and died in Vietnam. He was beloved and is greatly missed to this day, but I heard the respect that everyone had for him and his service. I learned to respect it as well. *Semper Fidelis* — Always Faithful. No matter what, I still feel that. That's the first part."

He paused again to gather his thoughts. "Then, I think the second part of it was that it was so different. Being in the Corps... It's an environment that can be brutal...dangerous. You live by your actions, and you're judged by what you do, not by anything you were or what you own, just by who you are and how you act. It's just about as far from wealth and privilege as you can get. I needed to test myself. I was starting to become something I'd spent my life hating. I was starting to become a rich playboy like my father, not caring who it affected."

Clara's mind raced, wondering what had happened, and Fitz must have seen it in her expression.

"Thank God, I actually hadn't hurt anyone yet. But...I realized that if I did, I might not care, and that scared me. My father wasn't a good man. There it is. And my mother wasn't much better. They both had every opportunity, every chance in life, and they squandered it all. I felt myself starting to do the same thing. So I went down to the local recruiter without telling anyone and signed on before anyone could try to talk me out of it." He gave a dry laugh. "Actually, I think my grandfather would have been more likely to try to bribe someone, anyone, but I made sure not to give him a chance. He earned his reputation for being ruthless the old-fashioned way, you know."

"Oh, I can definitely see that from spending time with him," Clara agreed.

Fitz leaned back into the soft couch and turned his head to keep looking at her, even though she thought he could probably only see her profile from that angle. "He likes you."

A warm blush crept up her neck and into her cheeks. "Is it so surprising?" she asked.

"Well, he doesn't like many people." Fitz smiled again, and it crinkled the corners of his eyes and made them gleam. "However, I never had any doubt that he would like you, my Clara Belle, since you are the most irresistible mix of sass, wit, beauty and kindness."

The blush that had been warm heated her face until she thought she could fry an egg on her cheeks, and she looked away. "Fitz!" she admonished.

"Oh, did I forget something?" he teased. "I was going to say sex appeal and gorgeous curves, but I hope to God my grandfather isn't noticing that about you. Although maybe you're right, honey. He's old, not dead."

Clara snorted. She couldn't help it. She was so surprised by his outrageous teasing that it just escaped her. Inelegant. Loud. She could have melted with embarrassment.

Fitz's grin widened even farther. "It appears I missed another attribute of yours, baby. An appalling oversight. I'm going to go ahead and add 'adorable when snorts' to the list."

"Oh my gosh!" she choked through her laughter, practically quaking with it. "You are incorrigible! I'm going to put Hope in her crib before I wake her up."

When she returned, he was still sitting in the same position, smiling to himself. He raised one dark eyebrow, and she couldn't help but smile in return.

"Can I ask you a question, too?" he asked, his face growing more serious.

"It's only fair," she answered, although she dreaded any number of questions — not because she didn't want to answer them, or tell him something. Instead, she dreaded hurting him by telling the truth then still leaving in two weeks.

"Are you happy, honey?"

She practically sighed with relief. "That's an easy one. Yes. I'm incredibly, deliriously happy here with you. It's just —"

He cut her off as if he knew what she was going to say. And heck, maybe he did. They *had* spent a great deal of time together, much of it in very trying circumstances. They were coming to know each other very well.

"Since that one was so easy, I think maybe I deserve a second one. You know, to be fair."

She hesitated, but she nodded her assent.

"I've been talking to Mac about this organization he's been involved with. It helps vets, especially wounded vets, with the more practical business and job-search related aspects of reintegrating into civilian life." He paused and she noticed that his chest rose and fell heavily, belying his otherwise casual position. "I think I would be in a unique position to do a lot of good for the group, and oddly enough, Drew and my grandfather both agree, so we're planning a gala in a couple of weeks." The slightest tremor in his voice was all it took for her to notice he was nervous — like, *really* nervous. "You helped me so much to get to a better place, especially with the Larsons. Would you come with me to the party, as my date?"

She turned toward him quickly, so that her knees bumped against his. "That sounds like an awesome opportunity to do a lot of good, and I'd be honored to be there with you."

She knew she was likely to feel totally out of her depth at a society gala, but there was no way she was going to say no to Fitz, not when this was obviously so important to him. It sounded like an amazing match for his skills and background, so what she'd said was honest. What she hadn't admitted — and tried not to admit even to herself — was that she really couldn't deny him anything. Somewhere between his eating her burnt grilled cheese and his gorilla impression, she'd fallen totally, completely, recklessly head-over-heels in love with him. Even knowing it was absurd to imagine she could ever fit in the world where he so obviously belonged, she hadn't been able to help herself.

His face lit up at her answer, and he gave her a crooked grin. "Thanks, baby. That means a lot to me." He looked like he might have said more, but there was a gentle knock, signaling that their dinner had arrived from the main house. No one rang the bell, careful not to wake the baby if she happened to be sleeping.

When Fitz returned, instead of carrying the usual bag with a delicious assortment of whatever the chef had put together for them, he held two pizza boxes and a six-pack of seltzer. Her heart skipped at how carefree he looked.

"Surprise," he said with a flourish, and she laughed.

"Mmm…I can smell it from here!" she enthused.

"One Hawaiian and one Meat Lovers, delivered fresh from Carducci's. Even though I personally maintain—and will be unlikely to have mind changed on this—that pineapple on a pizza a crime against pizza, nature and all that is holy."

Clara was stunned at his thoughtfulness. She'd mentioned, only once, that she missed getting Carducci's delivery to her old apartment. It was one of the few things she'd missed about her life in the city. He must have called them and asked her favorites. She opened her mouth, but no sound came out.

"I was going for sweet, but I'm thinking I ended up in Creepytown?" he guessed.

She shook her head, torn between crying and laughing. Her body decided for her, and an odd chortle escaped, making both of them laugh. "Definitely sweet. Fitz, it's just about the most thoughtful thing anyone has ever done for me." And it was. He'd listened— *really listened*—and remembered.

"Uh-oh. Should I stand back when I tell you I also have a cake from Sam's Pastries in the fridge, and a Blu-ray of your favorite eighties movie?" He was joking, but he also took a step backward.

If she hadn't already realized she loved him, she would have known it. Oh, not from what he'd done, although that was all incredibly nice. No, she would have known from the expression of anticipation and delight on his face as he'd told her. He'd done this for no other reason than to make her happy, and it obviously made him happy to watch her.

"You should come closer when you say something like that, not move farther away." She waggled her eyebrows playfully, keeping her tone light, but a definite spark of interest flashed in Fitz's expression. She felt his eyes on her like a caress, just for a moment, as if he were gauging her sincerity.

"I'll keep that in mind, honey." He winked and went into the kitchen, returning with a tray carrying glasses of seltzer, napkins and plates with one piece of each kind of pizza on both of them. He'd somehow even fit the promised movie, which was perched precariously on one corner.

She started to stand to help him, but he motioned her to stay where she was. The unforeseen byproduct of the forced rest of staying at the house and having everyone wait on her hand and foot was that he was also somewhat limited in what he did, and he'd made a complete recovery from his latest injuries. His leg still seemed to hurt him, but he said it was the best it had been since before his last mission.

"I've got this, baby. Let me take care of you," he said, and the words were a *double-entendre* to her, whether he'd intended it or not. Looking at the gleam in his blue eyes, she thought maybe he had. Whatever he'd intended, she felt a shiver of anticipation up and down the length of her spine.

They ate several pieces each of the glorious pizza, heavily laden with ooey-gooey cheese and the special spicy sauce she'd craved. When they'd finished, and Clara thought she couldn't eat another bite, Fitz brought out two pieces of cake and she found she had room after all.

At the first bite of velvety cake topped with creamy, luscious, melt-in-your mouth buttercream frosting, she moaned. She couldn't help it. When she looked over at Fitz, he had frozen with his fork halfway to his mouth. His expression had gone intent...almost predatory. All the desire he usually tried to hide blazed in the white-hot blue of his eyes.

"Clara," he breathed, the word almost torn from him. Somehow he managed to set both their plates and forks down almost instantly, so he could wrap his arms around her as he covered her mouth with his. He devoured her like a man who'd been starved, licking and nipping at her lips, stroking his tongue into her mouth, filling her with his taste, surrounding her with his warmth and clean scent.

She matched his intensity, her body suddenly on fire with need and passion, all stoked to life by Fitz and the feel of his hard body against her softness. She ran her hands up and down his back, tracing every tight muscle, then tangled her fingers in his short hair. It was incongruously soft against her fingertips, such softness and tenderness from such a hard man. She keened at the exquisite sensations assaulting her, and he deepened their kiss.

His sex rose, large and hard, against her hip, and she reveled in what she did to him — how she aroused him as much as he aroused her.

"You taste...you feel...so...*good*," he murmured between kisses, making her hair flutter with his breath. She shivered deliciously.

A cry pierced the air, tinny but distinct through the state-of-the-art baby monitor, and they both froze, Fitz swearing under his breath. Clara felt like swearing, too. It had been magical, and she didn't want it to end.

Fitz looked down at her from where he held himself on top of her, propping himself on his hands and arms. His expression was searching. "Are you...all right? I remember the doctor said something about six weeks, and he was here yesterday..."

She nodded, oddly embarrassed, which was silly, since they'd been groping each other a moment earlier. "He told me I'm doing well and cleared me for, uh, everything," she managed to choke out.

As Hope gave another wail, he pressed his forehead against hers. "I want you, honey," he groaned.

Not looking at him, but still feeling his masculine heat surrounding her, it was easy to respond. "I want you too, Fitz. *So much.*"

His sigh sounded relieved, and frustrated. "Take care of Hope, then come to my room." It wasn't an order, exactly, but she trembled at the command in his voice.

"*Yes*," she agreed, her voice husky. He released her, then stood across the room with his back to her as she hurried to tend to the baby.

As she changed and fed Hope, her mind was half on what they'd done and what she'd agreed to. Could she really go through with it? She loved him on every level, and she craved him — craved more of his body, his taste, his tenderness. She ached to be his and for him to be hers. That seemed to be what he offered, so part of her wanted to seize it with both hands. But would it hurt her more, having those beautiful memories, after she left?

She sighed and stroked Hope's silky head. She knew the answer. Darn right it would hurt more, but she couldn't imagine not ever being with him, not knowing him in every way — even if it would make everything ten times harder...a hundred times harder. She couldn't yet say the words, might never get the chance, so she had to at least show him with her body how much she loved him.

Once Hope was clean, dry, well-fed and sleeping again, with one last kiss on the sweet-smelling head, Clara laid her gently down in her crib and crossed back into her bedroom. Excitement and nervous anticipation permeated her, filling her, making her heart leap and her hands shake. Looking in the mirror as she hurried through brushing her teeth, she saw that her lips looked swollen...well-kissed. Her cheeks were flushed, and her hazel eyes were bright with anticipation. She was as ready as she'd ever be.

She practically ran to Fitz's room, not wanting to lose her nerve, and pushed his door open in a rush before she could talk herself out of it. The expression on his face as he turned to greet her, coming to meet her in three long strides and pulling her into his arms and into the room, made it worth it. He'd looked surprised, sexy and so tender that it made her heart pound. Then he was enveloping her again in his muscled arms and peppering her face with short kisses before he kissed her lips.

"I wasn't sure you'd come," he said, separating them but only slightly, just enough so he could look at her. She smelled toothpaste on his lips, and it was oddly endearing. They were both nervous, it seemed.

"I had to," she admitted, watching his reaction.

"Baby, baby...you drive me crazy with the way you look at me. Back at the cabin, I would feel your eyes on me, and it would make me wild with wanting you. I can't believe you're here, in my arms." He lowered his head to kiss her neck, soft, open-mouthed kisses that made her tremble with desire. "Knowing you better," he murmured, his voice slightly muffled against her neck, "I only want you more."

She let her head fall to the side to give him better access. "I'm yours."

Her words seemed to lower the floodgates that had been holding his desire in check and, with a sexy growl that made her nipples tighten, he lifted her right off her feet and carried her to the large bed. She thought he might throw her onto the soft surface, but instead he laid her down with surprising gentleness, stretching himself next to her, so close she could feel the heat of his body all along her side. She had only an instant to appreciate the feel of him in the new position before he bent to kiss her again. The kisses were long and passionate...drugging. He explored her mouth as if they had all the time in the world, stroking her body and nerves to a slow-building frenzy with his achingly tender touch. Her breathy moans were loud in the quiet room, and her body felt as if it were on fire. She couldn't believe how amazing he felt, even without having touched any of her main erogenous zones yet. The reason for his reticence became clear when he whispered his next question in a sort of low growl.

"Honey, is there anywhere I shouldn't touch you? Any part too sensitive?"

She flushed hot with embarrassment at his question, so tender and thoughtful—as she had learned the man himself was—and wished that she could have met him before her body had changed so much with pregnancy. She wanted to be perfect, and instead, she was barely healed. As she looked up at Fitz, lying propped up on one elbow, his face was almost haloed by the low light of the room, so handsome and concerned that it made her heart squeeze, and she knew that if she told him any part of her was off-limits or she'd changed her mind entirely, he would stop. The realization was exactly what she needed to overcome her sudden shyness.

"No," she breathed, "only…well, um, my breasts are tender and, ah, leaky…so if you don't want to touch them, I understand." She closed her eyes as she finished speaking, so she couldn't see his expression.

"Not want to touch them? Honey, watching you nursing the baby has been making me so hard I thought my dick would just burst out of my pants."

Her eyes flew open with surprise at his words, but she couldn't doubt the sincerity of his tone or his intent expression, almost pained.

"I'll be gentle, though. I want to make this feel so good for you, Clara."

With a sexy grunt that betrayed pure masculine need, he covered her mouth with his again, and gently stroked up her side with one warm hand until he covered one full, soft mound. With exquisite tenderness, he began to massage her gently, and she gasped at the sensation.

"Too much?" Fitz asked, instantly contrite.

Clara had always had sensitive nipples, but since she'd had Hope, they had become almost unbearably so at times. In the past, other men had been much too rough, so that she had started to avoid letting them be touched at all, but Fitz, with his gentle, careful caress was driving her crazy in a way she hadn't even known was possible.

"No, oh, no," she moaned, arching her back slightly to put her breast more fully into his hand, stilled on top of it. "So good, Fitz. Oh my goodness, like nothing I've ever felt."

His dark chuckle was her answer. "You're like nothing I've ever felt, Clara Belle," he whispered before he continued his light massage and drugging kisses, taking his time with both breasts until she was squirming and rubbing herself against him, her fingers tangled into his hair which had grown longer over the past few weeks.

When she was practically mindless with need from the feel of him, he tugged off her top, and deftly unhooked her bra with one hand. She gasped as her overheated skin met the cooler air, feeling her nipples, sensitized from his ministrations, hardened almost to the point of pain. Almost...but not quite. She realized that they felt so cool because they were damp, and she worried for a second that Fitz might find them off-putting. Instead, the expression on his face was almost reverent.

"God, you're gorgeous, honey." His eyes went dark, predatory. "But you're still wearing too many clothes," he growled. Before she'd even full registered his intent, he slid down from the foot of the bed to kneel in front of her, peeling off her socks, pants and underwear.

"Wh-what are you doing?" she asked, breathy with nerves...or was that excitement?

From his place between her thighs, Fitz's smile was roguish. "I think it's pretty obvious, isn't it?"

Clara tried to close her thighs. Fitz held them open firmly, but with gentle hands.

"You, uh, don't have to do that. I know, um, a lot of men really don't like it." Clara recalled very clearly that Brock had found the very idea of licking her distasteful, and her boyfriend in college hadn't seemed all that into it, either...had viewed it as more of a chore so that she'd stopped asking.

Fitz raised one eyebrow and she could have sworn his eyes glittered with warmth. "A lot of men are idiots... I've been dreaming of tasting your sweet little pussy since nearly the first moment I met you." Clara shifted, feeling herself go wetter, affected more by his dirty talk than she would have imagined. Without further warning, with a deep noise of pure lust, he bent his dark head to her core, licking her thoroughly from the bottom to the top of her slit, then circling around her sensitive bud. She bowed back her head at the intense pleasure of the sensation, so that she practically fell off the bed, thrashing her head back and forth on the bedspread. He continued to hold her in place with strong hands on her thighs, licking and sucking relentlessly, eliciting breathy little mewls and cries from her, building her toward something tall and shimmering, like no pleasure she'd ever felt. Then, suddenly, the peak washed over her like a giant wave, powerful and cleansing, and he rode it out with her, prolonging her pleasure with gentle laps and kisses until she collapsed backward, boneless and sated. She felt him move, and she had to prop her head up on her arms to watch him, almost shocked at the wanton way her thighs were still spread open but too satisfied to care.

He stood, rising tall and proud before her, but his expression was strangely nervous as he put his hands on the hem of his long-sleeved T-shirt. With a flash of understanding, it came to her. He was self-conscious about his scars.

Instantly, her lassitude transformed to tenderness, and she scooted back on the bed, holding his gaze. "I want to see you, Fitz. Feel your body against mine. *All* of your body," she urged, her voice low and throaty from her earlier cries.

The answering flare of desire in his eyes eclipsed the tension she'd seen there a moment earlier, although he still hesitated.

"I'm no prize, Clara...not much to look at these days."

She felt as if her heart might be melting at the uncertainty she read on his face, so incongruous for the tough, dependable ex-soldier. "Why don't you let me be the judge of that, hmm?"

He gave a ghost of a half-smile and pulled off his shirt, revealing his hard, muscular chest, smooth and scarred in equal parts. She sucked in a sharp breath, and his eyes looked hurt.

"Fitz...you're beautiful," she choked out, tracing every line of his chest with her eyes. She hated thinking about how much hurt had gone into him getting the scars, the agony behind every twisted and shiny dip in his skin, but she also saw the strength and determination it had taken for him to not only escape from the fire with his life, trying to rescue his fallen comrade, then to go through the lengthy, torturous recovery. That strength stunned her.

"If I'm beautiful, why are you crying, honey?" Fitz's question was soft in the quiet room.

She shook her head. "I'm not crying."

At his skeptical expression, she amended, "Well, not about you...being ruined or anything like that. I just... Your courage overwhelms me. Your body is spectacular, but your scars... I came so close to never meeting you...would never have met you if you didn't have the grit to go through such incredible pain in your recovery."

Fitz's expression was unreadable, some combination of tenderness and...something else. Something deeper?

But then it was gone, and there was a distinct, wry humor.

"If you like these scars, there're plenty more to see," he teased. She gave a watery smile.

"Bring it on, Sergeant Sexy," she returned, and his surprised bark of laughter rang out against the walls.

"I will bring it all for you, honey," he drawled, and she felt a delicate shiver go through her body, which didn't go unnoticed, if the heat that was back in his eyes were any indication. "Oh, damn...I forgot, uh..." Fitz looked suddenly uncomfortable, rubbing the back of his neck and making his chest muscles flex in a way that was so distracting she had a hard time focusing on what he was saying.

"Forgot?" she prodded.

"Stay right here...I have to get, um, protection."

Understanding dawned on her.

"I like that you weren't so sure of me that you have boxes of condoms in your drawer, but uh, I've been on birth control since my doctor's appointment a few weeks ago, and I'm clean, so..."

She trailed off, and his eyes darkened, the rapid rising and falling of his chest the only indication he'd heard her.

"God, baby...just when I think you couldn't get any sexier, you say something like that. I'm clean, too...been tested a hell of a lot. If you're sure?" The last question was strangled, almost torn from his throat.

She nodded, feeling suddenly like a sultry temptress. "I'm sure," she whispered.

Those words seemed to be all the permission he needed, and she watched avidly as he tore off his pants and boxers faster than she'd ever seen anyone remove any clothing. Whereas a minute earlier, she would have sworn she wouldn't be able to get aroused again any time soon, now her core went liquid with need. She had only a glimpse of his glorious, masculine body, his long, hard cock rising from a thatch of darker curls at his groin, before he pounced on her.

The feeling of his skin against hers, of his naked hardness against her naked softness, was amazing... exquisite. He covered her mouth with his and seated himself inside of her in one long stroke. She cried out at the sensation.

"Okay, baby?" He stilled, his face concerned as he asked.

Too overcome to speak, she just nodded. He seemed to understand, and a wicked smile spread across his face, almost feral in its masculine satisfaction. She felt filled as she never had been before, and she loved the sensation of utter closeness. He was a part of her, and she was a part of him. As he began to move in long, easy strokes, she gasped and panted, holding him to her and never wanting it to end. She ran her hands along his back, feeling smooth hot skin on his shoulders and the ridges of his scars lower. Her touch on his scars seemed to inflame him further, and he groaned.

"Baby, you're driving me crazy. You feel so goddamn amazing. You're so tight and hot, dripping for me, aren't you?"

Her breath hitched at his words, and she squeezed him with her legs, lifting her hips to meet each thrust more fully. "Yes, oh yes, Fitz!" She barely knew what she was saying, mindless with the pleasure of his touch.

He sped up gradually, giving her more and more speed just when she needed it. The soft sound of their bare skin meeting was rhythmic, steady in the quiet room, and she was so wet she could hear it as he drove into her. He changed the angle of his hips, just slightly, and she shuddered, crying out.

"You like that, hmm?" he asked, and she whimpered with need.

"Yes...so much!" she managed to gasp, and he sped up his thrusts, continuing to rub against that magical place inside her. She felt the spiral of deep pleasure build all over again, larger and all-encompassing, until she was panting and trembling, digging her heels into the muscles of his butt and her fingernails into his back.

"Are you going to come, honey? With your hot pussy all around my cock?" His words, combined with the power of his thrusts, sent her right over the edge into a free-fall into the total oblivion of pleasure, and she shook and undulated all around him.

Her orgasm seemed to set his off as well, and with one more long stroke and a hoarse cry, he pumped pulse after pulse of hot semen into her, filling her and setting off quakes with every movement. He collapsed on top of her, a heavy weight that she reveled in, and she squeezed his body with her arms and legs, kissing his cheek, scratchy with stubble and salty with sweat.

They were still and silent, except for their heavy breathing, for long moments. Clara couldn't take a deep breath, but she didn't care. She didn't care about anything except the magnificent man who was on top of her, still semi-hard inside her.

When Fitz caught his breath, he turned them so that he wasn't on top of her, but he was still pressing all along her naked side. "Honey...my God. You are incredible." He kissed her shoulder. "A deity of sensual delight." He kissed the side of her neck, and she laughed at his outrageous compliment.

"You're not so bad yourself, Lieutenant Lover," she answered, and loved how she could feel his surprised chuckle vibrating against her skin.

"Oh, honey…" he started, but stopped abruptly when they heard footsteps in the hall.

She checked the digital clock on the bedside table and saw that it was the usual time that Judith arrived to help. They had both obviously forgotten about her, and they held their breath until the steps passed, collapsing in relieved laughter when she'd passed.

"I can't believe we forgot Judith!" Clara said in a shocked whisper.

Fitz pulled her more tightly against him. "I can," he teased in a voice that rumbled in his chest.

"Fitz!" she laughed, playfully swatting his arm but not really wanting him to release her. It felt too good.

"Do you know what her being here means?" His tone was dark and sensual, making Clara shudder at the promise she heard there.

"N-no." She shook her head, her voice catching as she felt his mouth on her shoulder again.

"If we're quiet, we can do this all night," he groaned. To her delight, he set about proving it to her, over and over again.

Chapter Thirteen

Waking up with an armful of warm, sleepy, naked Clara was one of the most amazing and surreal sensations Fitz had ever experienced. He could tell from her slow, even breathing that she slept soundly. He wasn't surprised. He'd probably exhausted her. He could feel his own aches and pains, but it was worth it. Hell, it would have been worth a thousand times the pain to see his Clara coming apart around him and knowing that he'd brought her such pleasure.

He stroked his hand along her curvy side, marveling at how soft and creamy-smooth her skin was. What was more incredible was that she had chosen to be with him, hard and scarred as he was, inside and out. When she'd told him how much she loved his body, multiple times over the course of the night, he could tell she meant it. Waking up in that hospital bed so many months earlier, he'd wondered if he'd survive. Then when it was clear he would, he'd thought he might never be with a woman again. But Clara—his Clara

Belle—had not only accepted him but had shown him what lovemaking could truly be. It made everything he'd ever experienced in the past seem like a pale shadow, a pencil outline of a picture, when making love to her was the full oil painting, with vibrant colors, broad brushstrokes and an endless canvas.

The little hitch in her breath signaled she was awake, and Fitz was almost sorry he'd woken her—almost, but not sorry enough to keep his hands off her.

"Morning, honey," he said, turning her toward him so he could kiss her.

"Good morning," she answered. "What time is it?"

"Early," he reassured her. "Judith hasn't left yet, and Hope will probably sleep for a little longer, too."

"I should sneak back to my room," she said, but he could hear reluctance in her voice.

Fitz took a deep breath. He didn't want to scare her, but he thought that last night had changed things. He hoped, anyway. "Why don't you just have your clothes and things moved here? And we can ask Lars or Amber to pack up some more stuff from the cabin, too."

"What?" she asked, and the look of shock and surprise on her face was not what he'd hoped for.

"We could both stay in your room, if you'd prefer, since it's a little closer to Hope, although you know I have a monitor in here."

Clara scrambled out of bed, holding a sheet around her as if he hadn't seen and kissed every delectable inch of her body last night. Worse, as if she might be embarrassed.

"I'm not moving here. I'm still leaving in two weeks."

Her statement was like a bucket of ice-water over his head. He felt numb, then he felt angry and really, really hurt.

"I thought...after last night things had changed," he said a little lamely.

She didn't look at him as she spoke, letting some of her hair fall forward to partially cover her face. "Nothing has changed, Fitz. I still don't belong here."

He sat up. "That's not true, honey. You belong with me, just like I belong with you."

He swore as a little wail rent the quiet air. Baby Hope was awake and hungry.

The hazel eyes she turned toward him were sad — anguished, even — but determined. "I just can't," she whispered, and hurried out, wearing only his bedsheet.

Clara hated knowing she'd hurt Fitz. He'd never said it, but she'd seen it on his face before she'd turned away from him. It was there in his manner, too. He remained funny and sweet, gentle with Hope and with her, but he'd put up an invisible wall — a wall that only came down at night when they made love. She'd thought he might not want to make love to her again, but instead, he made love to her every night. He came to her room and took her so passionately and with such total abandon that it felt as if he were trying to show her how he felt on a primal level, to wear down her resistance with his body. And it was working.

She'd never felt so torn about anything. She, who was usually so decisive, was now wondering whether leaving was really the right thing after all. And so the days flashed by, almost feeling as if they were in fast-forward, full of tension and indecision on her part. The nights passed too quickly, as well, but for a different reason — because she never wanted them to end. She knew, without a doubt, that she'd never feel this way about another man. Fitz had crawled right into her heart and filled it so that there would never be room for another. But she knew how these things worked now. She would never again be naïve enough to believe that someone like Colin Fitzhugh would be permanently happy with a former paralegal for a law firm who was now an unemployed single mother, not even sure of the next steps she wanted to take with her life.

The morning of the gala was chilly, a few flurries swirling outside the windows, and she was restless. Fitz had been even more passionate than usual the night before, and more distant than ever in the morning. Always, she saw the flicker of hurt and self-doubt in his beautiful eyes. Remembering it now made her heart physically ache in her chest.

She had awakened to the feeling of Fitz kissing down her side, her body still bare from their lovemaking the night before, working his way to the warm juncture of her thighs.

"You're insatiable!" she'd laughed sleepily. *"You had me three times last night."*

"Want you three more times this morning," he'd replied, his gravelly voice muffled by the comforter. *"Is that going to be a problem, baby?"* His growly tone had made her give a little shiver of desire.

"Nope...no problem here," she'd breathed, and he'd nipped her skin, between her hip and her butt, soothing it immediately with a kiss.

"Hey!" she'd protested.

"Sorry...couldn't resist," he'd answered, not sounding contrite at all. She'd planned to complain again but then he'd settled between her legs and had begun to lap at her core and she hadn't been able to think of anything else.

"Fitz! Oh my goodness..." She'd let her legs fall open almost without conscious thought, and he'd taken full advantage.

"Tastes. So. Fucking. Sweet," he'd grunted against her, the rumbling enhancing her pleasure. She'd thought she had been worn out from the night before, when he'd been like a madman, taking her over and over until she'd practically collapsed, but now he'd barely started touching her before he'd been driving her right up the height of ecstasy again.

"Fitz!" she'd screamed as he sent her over the edge, the pleasure sneaking up like a wave that turned into a tsunami, and she'd tightened her thighs unconsciously, holding him in place.

When she'd realized what she'd done, she'd loosened her grip and sat up suddenly, throwing the covers off of them. *"Oh my gosh! Are you okay? Can you breathe?"*

Fitz had looked up at her with a chuckle, his lips still glistening with her juices. *"I'll admit I was getting a little short on oxygen there, honey, but what a way to go,"* he'd teased, and she'd thrown a small pillow at him. He'd ducked so she'd missed his head.

"Not funny!" she'd retorted, scrabbling around behind her to find another pillow, but coming up empty. She'd flipped over to crawl up the corner of the bed — they must have knocked almost all of the pillows off the night before — when she'd heard Fitz's deep growl in her ear.

"Don't worry, baby...there was no way I was going to miss this." He'd grabbed her hips, gently but firmly, driving himself inside of her from behind, all the way up to the hilt.

She'd moaned.

"*Too much?*" he'd asked, pulling back slightly.

"*No...so good,*" she'd gasped, and he'd driven himself back inside of her.

"*Been dreaming of doing that again all night...just waited,*" he'd grunted and spoken in time with his thrusts, "*for you...to wake...up.*" Clara had braced herself on her elbows, the slight change in position making him go even deeper with each stroke. Each time he'd moved, it had rubbed her sensitive nipples lightly against the sheet, driving her pleasure to new heights.

"*You're so deep,*" she'd ground out the words on an exhale. "*Feels amazing.*"

Fitz had made a sound suspiciously like a full-on roar behind her. "*Wanna go so deep you'll never get me out of you, baby...never forget.*" His rhythm had sped, grown frenzied, until she'd been nearly bumping the headboard. He hadn't slowed, and she hadn't wanted him to.

"*Tell me you're mine,*" he'd demanded, and the possession in his tone had made her channel squeeze tight around his length. "*Right now, you're mine!*"

"*I'm yours,*" she'd agreed. "*Yours, yours, yours...*" she'd continued, breaking off in a loud cry as pleasure, so wild it had been nearly painful in its intensity, had torn through her. She'd heard Fitz bellow behind her before he'd emptied himself into her, filling her with his hot essence.

He'd collapsed, spooning her, with her back pulled tightly to his front, and he'd buried his face in the place between her neck and shoulder, inhaling deeply. The silence had stretched long after they had both caught their breath again.

"*Fitz,*" she'd started tentatively. "*You know —* "

"I know. It's later than I thought," he'd cut her off, his voice nearly toneless. *"Hope will be up any minute, and it's a big day today."*

He'd turned away from her quickly, but before he had, she'd caught a glimpse of his eyes.

She bundled little Hope into a fuzzy sleeper, along with several blankets, and took her outside. Clara had her cell phone and she'd thought she might call Amber or Lars, just to talk things through. Instead, her feet, almost with a mind of their own, carried her to the main house. She took the ornate elevator up to the third floor, which was Pat's domain, and Roger met her at the door.

"Miss Clara and Miss Hope. What a lovely surprise," Roger intoned in his very proper voice, the one she thought he'd probably practiced as a young butler until it sounded just right, but she could tell he was genuinely pleased to see them. As soon as Hope spotted the two older men, she cooed, her little eyes wide as she watched their every move.

"Come here, girlie," Pat said in an ornery voice from the massive armchair in the corner near the window that he favored. "And bring the wee lass," he added in an imperious tone.

Clara smiled at the theatrics. *My goodness but these two are big on theatrics!* Still, she dutifully unwrapped Hope and carried her over to Fitz's grandfather. He held her for a moment, but when she spit up, he was only too happy to pass her to Roger, who wiped her up and cradled her like a pro.

"What's got you looking so down in the mouth, girlie? I bet it's that rascal grandson of mine and the tiff you two had a couple of weeks back, eh?"

Pat's question surprised her at first, but when she looked into the faded blue eyes that were still so very shrewd, she realized she should have known he'd recognize her mood. He and Fitz were alike that way.

"I wouldn't call it a tiff," she hedged.

"Ha!" the older man crowed. "I told Roger you'd had a falling out. He told me to mind my own business, which of course I couldn't do. Roger, didn't I tell you?"

The butler's voice was dry as he replied, though the effect was somewhat spoiled by the gurgling baby he held. "Yes, sir. I do recall you said something to that effect."

Pat laughed, his wizened face crinkling with glee, before he turned his laser focus back on Clara. "So, what's the problem? It's obvious, plain as the nose on my face, that the two of you care for each other. Why don't you get started on giving me some more great-grandchildren?"

His comment startled a laugh from her. "You do not beat around the bush, do you, Pat?"

"Never have," Pat confirmed, sounding proud. "I was too damn stubborn and focused on getting my own way when I was younger, and now I'm just too damn old to take the time."

Clara heaved a deep breath, wondering whether she was actually about to ask advice from Fitz's own grandfather. Then she just did it.

"I'm not like you," she said.

"How so?" Pat asked mildly.

"You and Fitz, er, Colin and Drew and Lana. You all belong here. No one questions your right to be here, or spreads stories about you. I'm...different."

"I see," Pat answered, and tapped one bent finger against his chin. "This is about you being hurt by that shady ex-boyfriend of yours."

"What? No!" Clara denied, taken aback by his comment.

"Well, girlie, you belong here as much as the rest of us. Sure, my grandchildren were born into this family and the wealth we'd built up, but it wasn't easy for them. They paid a steep price for it, and they didn't always even have the benefit of it from their parents. But I...I was born poor — the kind of poor I think and pray you don't understand, wondering where our next meal would come from, wondering whether we might starve. I had a great idea and some phenomenal luck, and I built everything we have, with the help my dear Flora." He paused, and his voice softened as he spoke his late wife's name. "Do you think Twin Cities society wanted *us* in it?" he demanded. "Two upstart Irish immigrants with more money than most of them put together?"

Clara realized he was waiting for an answer. "No?" she guessed.

Pat cackled again. "You bet your sweet patootie, they didn't!" He wheezed in amusement at the memory. "We made them accept us. We wore them down, like rivers flowing over mountains. We just kept doing well until they couldn't ignore us, and we joined the country clubs, the social clubs, went to all the best parties, sent our sons to the best schools."

He looked at Clara again, and she was surprised by the sadness and regret she saw in his eyes, which somehow seemed older all of a sudden.

"That was our choice and our path, God help us. We tried to do right, but maybe we did more wrong than right, especially with Colin's father, Bertie. I'm only grateful his children forgave us." Clara touched his arm, unable to stop herself from comforting the old man.

He covered her hand briefly with his, and she felt how thin his skin was, how twisted and swollen his joints were. Her heart squeezed in sympathy.

He seemed to shake off his melancholy and continued. "Point is, no one belongs one place or another. We make our own destinies. Hell, Colin has spent almost his entire adult life outside of this society entirely, by choice. So if you think he gives a rat's ass about some petty, unkind rumors spread by a sniveling society lawyer, think again." He leveled another gaze on her, and she shifted uncomfortably under it. "I know my grandson. He has his faults, but disloyalty isn't one of them. So the question is whether you're strong enough, whether he means enough to you, to face your own fears and insecurities."

Clara's mouth hung open, and she knew she ought to be offended. She *was* offended. At least, she thought she was. But then again, maybe he was right. She shut her mouth with a snap. *Had* she been telling herself it was best for all of them because she didn't want to embarrass herself and Fitz in front of the society that Brock represented to her? She thought about everything Fitz had done and said. She knew he'd believed that he was unworthy of her, but he'd been courageous enough to overcome that. Was she really going to deny them a possible lifetime of happiness by doing any less?

A satisfied chuckle recalled her to where she was — sitting with Pat and Roger, and Hope who had drifted off into a happy sleep.

"Gotcha there, didn't I?" Pat prodded, and she felt a smile curve her lips in spite of herself.

"You sure did," she agreed.

"This gala means a lot to him, you know." Clara knew he was talking about Fitz. "He swore to me he'd never use our influence again unless it was for good — complete and utter good. It's going to be a big night for him, and it's a big deal that he chose to ask you to be by his side."

Clara had known it seemed important to Fitz, but she hadn't realized just how important.

"With the right woman as his partner, there's nothing a man can't do, nowhere he can't go." Pat's voice went quiet as he continued. "Then again, anywhere he goes with her, whether it's a one-bedroom apartment with a Murphy Bed, a fancy custom-built palace or even a cabin in the woods, feels like paradise."

Clara stood, feeling suddenly lighter. He was right. He was so totally right that she couldn't believe she hadn't seen it. "I have to go get ready," she said.

Pat and Roger exchanged the look of two old friends who were pleased with themselves.

"You go on, Miss Clara. We'll bring Miss Hope back to the old house a little later. Isn't Judith coming earlier than usual tonight to assist?" Roger asked.

Clara nodded. It was like they were omniscient. She secretly thought Roger might have bugged some of the rooms. *For efficiency, mind you.* He was the soul of discretion. "She's coming slightly before five."

"Go on, then!" Pat shooed her. "What are you waiting for?"

She hurried out, intent on getting ready, and barely heard the conspiratorial laugh the two old men exchanged.

* * * *

Fitz had left earlier, saying something about loose ends to tie up. He'd been very clear that he'd be back to pick her up around five o'clock, though, so she should be ready.

She'd gone out to the Mall of America one day the previous week to pick out her dress. Fitz had made an appointment with one of the personal shoppers at one of the large department stores there, and she'd tried on several evening gowns, all in her size and chosen with an eye to flatter her curves. She hadn't known quite what to expect, especially when he'd asked her permission to send a photo to the shopper in advance, but Betty Jean had a true gift. Not one dress she'd picked for Clara had looked bad. Given her short stature, pale coloring and ample chest and hips, Clara considered the other woman somewhat of a miracle worker...or fairy godmother. She'd even been tickled by the individual phones in the dressing rooms, which were the size of her entire cabin in Cameronville. Those phones were over-the-top, but fun. She'd felt like a princess. The only part of the shopping trip that had bothered her had been the end. Fitz had somehow arranged it so that he'd prepaid for whatever dress she chose, so they hadn't let her pay. She didn't know exactly how much it was, so she'd have to call the store before she wrote him a check.

Now, unzipping the frosted garment bag in her closet and looking again at the dress she'd finally chosen, she vowed that whatever the price was, it was worth it. The fabric was soft and silky but draped beautifully, and it was a vibrant, deep emerald green that made her eyes look darker and more striking. It did something to bring out the red in her hair, too, and made her skin look almost ethereal instead of just plain pale like it sometimes did. It was simply cut, but the very simplicity of its lines made it stand out. She couldn't wait for Fitz to see her in it.

She hung the long gown from the top of the bathroom door, so any wrinkles that had managed to get into it in transit would be steamed out while she showered. She'd splurged a little at the makeup store, too, getting soap and lotion in her favorite scent, and some of the fancy hair product that she hadn't bothered with in months. It turned her hair from fuzzy curls that tended to frizz to sleek, shiny curls that bounced. Well, as long as there wasn't too much humidity. If she got rained on, there was no hope, but at least she could start the evening with frizz-free hair.

Satisfied with her hair and skin, she took her time with her makeup, too. It felt good to get all gussied up again, and she realized with shock that she hadn't done this once since leaving the law firm. An impish smile looked back at her from her reflection at the thought that Fitz might not recognize her. When she'd finished her face, she surveyed the results, and she definitely liked what she saw. Her eyes stood out, her skin looked flawless and her lips made everything pop. She'd even used eyeshadow, something she rarely ever did, to add a little bit more of a sultry touch. She felt gorgeous as she sauntered with her dress to the other room.

She had a little extra time, so she did something else she hadn't done in months. She read, reclined on her bed in just her black lace bra and panties, paired with control-top silk pantyhose since she wanted to smooth all the wobbly baby-holding bits at least a bit. Finally, she slid into the dress, and slipped on the low-heeled black leather pumps she'd bought. Clara finished the look with her mother's pearl necklace and earrings that Mac had gotten from Lars the week before when he'd made a trip up to Cameronville.

When she heard a rustling, she peeked next door to Hope's room and was gratified to see the look of surprise on Judith's face. The other woman was older, very motherly and every bit as nice as Fitz had promised. Clara really liked her, and the feeling seemed to be mutual. Best of all, Judith really seemed to like Hope. Clara hoped that Judith might stay for at least a while longer, then she nipped that thought in the bud. Gosh, she was getting ahead of herself.

Now, Judith's kind eyes lit up. "Beautiful, Clara. Just lovely!" she exclaimed. She held Hope up, whose eyes had gone wide. "Doesn't your mama look pretty, Hope?" Judith asked.

Hope gurgled and they both laughed. "I'm going to take that as a yes, sweet pea," Clara answered.

"Do you want me to take a picture, for your brother and your friend...Amber, is it?"

Clara was touched that the older woman remembered Amber's name, and what she'd mentioned about Lars before. "They would love that. They were both sad not to be here," Clara answered.

Like a pro, Judith managed to hold the baby and Clara's cell phone to take several flattering pictures, which Clara sent right off to Lars and Amber with silly messages. As she'd typed to Amber, now she had photographic proof that she looked *good*. She thanked Judith.

"I hope you have a great time," the other woman said, stepping back with a kind smile, "and for such a good cause, too." The admiration in her voice was obvious. Clara was going to say more, but the sound of the front door made her heart leap into her throat.

Fitz was home.

Chapter Fourteen

Fitz wasn't sure how he felt about wearing his dress blues again after so long. He felt like a snake who'd shed his skin, then had to put it back on again. The clothes fit his body, but they didn't fit *him* like they had before. So much had changed for him since then—battle, tragedy, pain, slow recovery, then finally, joy and love. He'd admitted it to himself at last in the morning, right after he'd left her, sleepy and sated, well-loved by her man. He loved Clara with all that was left of his pieced-together body and soul. He loved Hope as well, as much as if she were his own daughter, and he couldn't imagine a life without the two of them.

He knew Clara was afraid of society, of being ostracized and hurt again, but he hadn't shown her clearly enough that he didn't care about Twin Cities' society or its elite. He was using his influence for good with the charity that he and Mac both believed in, but after tonight, he could back off on his involvement and they could make their home anywhere—away from the

Twin Cities, maybe even away from Minnesota entirely. He'd give Clara the choice. As long as he had her and Hope, he knew they'd be happy.

He was making some progress with her. He could feel it. Every night, she seemed more and more open. And every morning, she'd been more reluctant for him to put up the wall between them. After tonight's gala, when they were alone, he'd tell her everything — man up and put it all out there for her to take or refuse. He hoped — and prayed — that she'd take him.

He tugged at the collar of his jacket as he entered the front entryway, so he was looking down momentarily. When the hint of a soft, swishing noise reached his ears, he raised his chin and saw a vision. It was Clara, still looking like the angel he'd initially mistaken her for, but he'd never seen her look like this before.

Her dress appeared as though it had been poured onto her, lovingly hugging her every curve, and the deep green color contrasted with her skin, making it glow like the creamy inside of an iridescent seashell. And her hair... Gone was the fuzzy mop he'd so come to enjoy, replaced by sleek, red curls that exploded in an artfully messy riot around her face. She was glowing all over, almost shining from within with happiness, and he couldn't tear his eyes away from her.

"What do you think?" she finally asked, her luscious red lips curving into a half-smile.

"You look exquisite. Elegant but sexy as hell. And if you don't hurry, I'm going to pick you up and carry you back upstairs so I don't have to break anyone's arm for looking at you tonight."

A full smile spread across her face now. He'd thought she couldn't look any lovelier, but he'd been wrong. Happy Clara in a ballgown was even more devastating. He was afraid what might happen if she laughed. Would he have a heart attack? If so, he'd die happy.

"Then I'd better move it," she said on a laugh, coming down the grand staircase carefully but quickly. When he looked up into her eyes again, he saw frank appreciation there. "You don't clean up so badly yourself, Sergeant Sharp."

He made a face. "What happened to Lieutenant Lover?"

She reached the bottom of the stairs, and he smelled something delicious and delicate. The scent suited her perfectly. And he'd be lucky if they made it out of this house without him tearing her gown off.

"Oh, I'd like to see him again later," she teased, but there was a sexy glint to her hazel eyes. And maybe it was wishful thinking, but he could have sworn he saw something else he hadn't seen before — something deeper and more permanent.

He lifted her hand to his lips, drawing out the contact of his gloved hand on her satiny skin. He let his lips linger for a moment longer than was necessary and she blushed.

He held out his arm formally, which she took with a flourish, and they stepped out onto the front porch. He couldn't help but feel a warm satisfaction at her swift intake of breath when she saw the gleaming antique car he'd parked out front.

"Is she beautiful?" he asked, proud of his handiwork.

"Beautiful doesn't do her justice. My goodness! What is she, a Rolls-Royce Phantom?"

She could have knocked him over with a feather, he was that surprised. "Yes, a Phantom III. I'm impressed,

Ms. Olafson. Very impressed." How many other wonderful things were there to discover about her? He couldn't wait to find out.

Her grin was sassy. "I'd like to take credit, but I come from a family of closet gearheads. My grandfather, father and brother all liked antique cars, so I've spent many a summer Saturday morning walking around some parking lot or other, listening to old men gun their engines."

"I'll bet you revved everyone's engines, honey," he teased, waggling his eyebrows.

"Wouldn't *you* like to know?" she returned, matching him tit for tat. "What's the story behind this lovely lady? They're pretty rare."

"Ah, we call her Florette, after my grandmother. She and my grandfather had always joked, after they saw one driving down their street, that they'd buy one for themselves when they made it. For her sixtieth birthday, we found one up for auction and fixed it up together. Well, with Roger's help. He's a whiz. You'd never guess." It felt good to talk about his grandmother...about his family. Fitz had come to realize that, by escaping them, he'd also cut himself off emotionally from a lot of what made him who he was. Sure, he didn't have to face the unhappy memories, but he also missed talking about the happy times.

"Oh, I think your Roger has untold depths."

Fitz raised his eyebrow. "I knew you were a good judge of character. Shall we?"

He opened the door for her and got her settled in. When he came around, Judith had come out with baby Hope to wave them off.

The venue wasn't very far away, so they arrived quickly. They were so early that the valets were just setting up, so he waved them off and pulled into one of the front spots. Florette always looked good out front at parties. It meant a Fitzhugh was in attendance. He knew he should probably have kept to his rule from younger days, to arrive later and bring the party with him, but times had changed. This wasn't something he was doing for fun. He *wanted* everything to go well. He and Mac had been working on this event for the past few weeks, and they stood to raise enough money to make a huge difference in the lives of a large number of veterans. Appearing as the prodigal son at a big party and turning on the Fitzhugh charm was the least he could do to ensure that happened.

As they walked into the ballroom, a beautifully restored room in one of the most historic Victorian-era hotels in the area, appreciation was plainly written on Clara's face. She did a slow turn, craning her neck to see the flowers and glassware placed all around, the tower of champagne flutes, the small band tuning their instruments.

"Fitz, it's beautiful!" she enthused, turning a shining face toward him. "It feels like a decadent turn-of-the-century garden party, in the middle of November."

He'd hoped she'd like it, but he felt suddenly self-conscious. "They did a good job, didn't they? Mac's been way more involved than I have. I'm just the big name to draw the crowd." He tugged at his collar again. "Actually, Drew and Lana were surprisingly helpful, too. When I mentioned it to them, they wanted to help, and Lana has used the caterers for a bunch of parties in the past."

Her genuine surprise and happiness—for him—was evident. "That's just awesome, Fitz. I'm so glad that they're supportive and worked with you on this."

"Speak of the devil, here's Mac now."

Mac walked over to them, all smiles. He might not have been born into Twin Cities society, but he sure had gotten the charm bit down. At Clara's welcoming expression, Fitz felt a twinge of what he thought might be...jealousy? He wasn't totally sure, because he'd seldom experienced it before and only with Clara. Whatever it was, he didn't like it.

Mac let out a low whistle when he saw Clara. "You look radiant, Clara. Wow! Fitz will be the envy of every man here."

Fitz wanted to glower at the man, but at least Mac had said something to make it clear that he understood Clara was Fitz's.

"Thanks," Clara answered, her cheeks growing a little pink. She couldn't hide her emotions or her blushes worth a damn, and he loved it. "You look pretty spiffy as well."

Mac preened, brushing an imaginary piece of something off the shoulder of his own dress uniform. "Thank you for noticing." He grinned, but it didn't quite reach his eyes.

"How's everything going?" Fitz asked, worried.

Mac shook his head and waved his hand to encompass the room. "Oh, everything's good for the most part. The room looks fantastic, the different crews and groups are all here and setting up. We had a snag with the caterer..."

"Oh?" Fitz prompted.

"Yeah, one of them was acting disrespectful toward your sister, so I fired him on the spot, but she's all bent out of shape over it."

His face was animated when he spoke, irritated. Mac was generally easy-going to the point of being considered too laid back by some, but he was irritated about Lana. *Very interesting.*

Mac rushed to reassure Fitz. "Everything's fine with the food, though. It's a beautiful spread. I think we're going to pull this off with style, man."

"Great. Sounds like you have everything in hand, but let me know if you need me," Fitz said, meaning it.

"Of course. But if you just stand there and look pretty, I think that'll be fine," Mac teased.

"Hey!" Clara protested with a laugh, and he realized she'd thought Mac had been teasing her.

"I'm sorry to tell you, honey, but he was talking to *me*," Fitz clarified as Mac sauntered off. Fitz loved seeing her eyes light up as she gave an elegant snort of amusement.

In spite of his outward calm—and good gracious, nobody did suave and cool like Colin Fitzhugh—Fitz seemed fidgety. He shifted his weight from one foot to the other, and he kept adjusting his collar, his lapel, even his sleeve. With a burst of insight, she realized he was nervous. *Really* nervous.

She leaned close, standing on her tiptoes to get closer to his ear, and whispered, so no one nearby would hear, "It's going to be perfect. I trust you."

Fitz's smile was sheepish. "Is it that obvious?"

"Only to me," she answered.

"I've been away from this life a long time, so it isn't as comfortable for me anymore. Time was, I'd go to several of these galas a week, and party all the other nights. Now, it's really about the charity. Drew stepped up and got some amazing donations for the silent auction, and we've had a ton of sponsors and RSVPs. There's no reason anything should go wrong, but...I just keep thinking about the soldiers the money we raise is going to help. Any amount we miss out on would have gone to help a guy like Mac or me, or even the widow of a guy like Abe Larson, reenter civilian life with a job and the pride of supporting his or her family." Fitz's blue eyes blazed with conviction and empathy as he spoke, and Clara loved him even more.

"You're a good man, Colin Fitzhugh. The best." She squeezed his arm, and would have said more, but the first wave of early arrivals had started to filter into the ballroom.

Fitz flashed her a dazzling smile. If she hadn't known otherwise, she never would have guessed he was anything other than a ridiculously handsome, brilliantly charming society playboy, about to have a great time. "It's showtime, honey," he said quietly through the smile, his tone dry.

She curved her lips into a smile that she hoped might come within the same ballpark as his for wattage and turned to be introduced to the first guests, an older couple decked out to the nines.

Fitz played the part perfectly. He was everything all the guests had come to see—charming, funny, witty, attentive, relatable but oh-so-glamorous. His uniform emphasized his very real service to his country, while the surroundings were a reminder of upscale opulence and the society he was born into. He made light of his own experiences as a Marine and instead focused on others, touching just heavily enough on the danger and sacrifices to be moving, but not so much that anyone wasn't having a good time.

She could tell by the occasional tightening of his lips or the carefully blank expression he pasted on from time to time, that it wasn't as easy as he made it look, and that some things that people asked or said were distasteful to him. Still, no one else would have noticed.

All through the evening, he held her hand on his arm, and she moved at his side. He introduced her to everyone they met and made it blatantly obvious that she was his. She could practically feel the heated whispers on her bare back as they walked away from each group, and speculation probably ran rampant as to what she was to him, but Clara was warmed every time by the proud look of possession in his eyes. He seemed not to care what people made of their relationship beyond knowing that they were together.

The cocktail hour portion of the event was just ending, and people were making their way to their tables for the dinner, when a man bumped into her arm. As she turned, her heart dropped all the way from her chest to the floor at the familiar face. *Brock*. She would have said he looked handsome, but she knew better. The slick, polished exterior held nothing of substance within, only malice and arrogance.

His pleasant expression changed to something much nastier when he realized it was her. "What the hell are you doing here, Clara?" he demanded on a hiss. "Find someone else to try to trick into marrying you with the story of a brat that probably isn't even his?" His face registered disdain bordering on distaste, as if she were rotting garbage instead of the woman he'd worked with for years and dated for over six months. She wondered again how his thin veneer of civility had ever fooled her. He leaned closer, and her eyes almost watered with the alcohol fumes on his breath. He'd always been one to enjoy a good open bar. "Or did you come here to find me? I thought I made it extremely clear that we had nothing more to say to each other."

Even though she told herself she didn't care, it was still a nightmare seeing him. When she tried to speak, to tell him every brilliantly cutting insult she'd come up with, all of them had fled from her mind and she was just embarrassed — ashamed of the scene they were beginning to make, not for herself, but because she didn't want to be the thing that ruined Fitz's evening.

Fitz stepped forward from where he'd been standing on her other side, and the look he turned on Brock was thunderous...murderous. "Clara is my guest and very close friend. I'm not sure who you are, though."

The steely glint in Fitz's eyes should have warned Brock, but her ex-boyfriend seemed either too arrogant or too tipsy to care. "Brock Templeton. I'm a partner at Carter, Lacey & Shaw LLP. We have a table." He puffed out his chest slightly. "I'm also a personal friend of the Fitzhughs."

Fitz quirked an eyebrow in surprise. "That's odd, since I'm a Fitzhugh and I don't know you at all — or like you, for that matter."

Brock spluttered in outrage, rendered speechless, for once.

"I checked the guest list personally, as a matter of fact, looking for your name to make sure you weren't on it." He looked at Clara apologetically. "I'm sorry, honey. Some of the people who sponsored tables didn't give individual names."

Clara was confused. Why was Fitz apologizing to her when it was her weasel of an ex-boyfriend who was ruining his event?

"I wanted to make sure this man wouldn't be here to bother you and that you never had to see him again, if you didn't want to," Fitz explained. Something in his eyes was so gentle, so deep, that it made her breath hitch.

"Now, see here!" Brock protested loudly. Clara noticed that a large circle of onlookers had formed, and they looked back and forth between the trio in open curiosity. "I'm a Templeton, and just as much a member of Twin Cities' society as you are. We trace our roots back much further than your Irish grandparents," Brock sneered.

Fitz raised his eyebrows. While he didn't get visibly upset, Clara noticed that he balled his fists at his sides. "Is that so?" he asked in a dangerously soft tone.

"Given your background, it's not surprising you'd associate with a cheap slut who thinks she's better than she is," Brock continued, oblivious to Fitz's growing rage. Several people gasped and looked at Clara. She tried to stay stoic, but she felt a hot flush rise all over her chest, neck and face. How had she ever been with that worm?

For a second, she thought Fitz was going to level Brock with a punch. She turned her head and saw that Mac, Drew and Lana had come to the front of the circle of onlookers, which now appeared to include most of the party. Mac's expression was dark as well, and he looked ready to leap on Brock.

To her surprise, Fitz took a deep, calming breath and spoke instead of throwing a punch. "Clara Olafson, to whom I can only assume you very crudely referred, is the kindest, funniest, most beautiful and caring person I have ever had the great pleasure to know." He turned and took both of her hands into his, raised them to his lips and kissed them.

Clara's heart actually fluttered in her chest, but her attention was diverted by something Brock said in a tone that, in his inebriated state, he probably thought was under his breath, but which was distinctly audible to everyone close by.

"Don't know about kind or funny, but she sure is damn lucky to have survived her pregnancy."

A sick feeling of dread rose within Clara as the last piece fell into the puzzle of her preeclampsia, which could have so easily ended tragically for her and Hope.

"*What* did you say?" Fitz demanded in a low, menacing voice, taking a step closer to Brock, who still seemed mostly oblivious. He never had been able to hold his alcohol, and he must have had an awful lot.

"Just…I heard that she was so stupid she was taking something that raised her blood pressure instead of lowering it, out in her little secret cabin."

When Fitz took another step forward and Mac came in close as well, it seemed to finally sink in to Brock that he might have spoken out of turn. His gaze darted around uncomfortably, and he smoothed his bowtie.

"Mac, did you hear that?" Fitz's voice was quiet, dangerously quiet.

The pilot gave a curt nod. "I heard it, and I recorded it. I'm calling the police."

"What? There's no need to call the police over a stupid bitch who couldn't keep her legs closed—" Brock's whiny tone was cut off by Fitz and Mac, in silent assent, leading Brock to a side-room with no small amount of force. Clara almost went to help, but she felt rooted to the spot, stunned.

"…hands off me!" She heard Brock's nasally tone— *how did I never notice how whiny the man is?*—as if through a long tunnel.

"…like to put my fist on you but don't wanna give you any standing at all with the police." She vaguely heard Fitz's angry voice before a door closed behind the men.

"Well, let's not let that...uh, interlude detract from tonight's purpose, okay?" Drew's overly hearty tone was a bit forced, but it seemed to get the guests who had gathered to dissipate somewhat.

Clara was startled to feel the soft touch of Fitz's sister, Lana's, hand on her shoulder as Drew martialed the guests away from her.

"Sorry...didn't mean to startle you. You just looked like you really needed to sit down." Lana's voice was quiet, cultured and apologetic as she led Clara to one of the sumptuous loveseats with cream-colored upholstery scattered up against the walls of the room.

"Thanks." Clara knew that her smile was weak, but Lana returned it. Up close, Clara realized that she had the same eyes as her brother. Kind eyes, in spite of all of her elegance.

"I just...can't believe he tried to physically harm me and our baby. I knew he didn't want her...but to try to poison me, or at least to make me so sick that I might die and Hope could have died... My God." Clara didn't even know how to feel.

Lana's expression was agonized. "Some people are just rotten inside, like a beautiful, juicy apple filled with a hollow, squishy center of black mold and worms."

The vehemence of her tone surprised Clara, and she wished she knew the other woman better, well enough to ask more. Lana continued before she could decide what else to say.

"I'm so grateful that my brother was there to help you—and Mac, even if he is an ass." Lana, who had taken the chair right next to Clara, took her hand as well. "I've never seen my brother so happy as he is with you."

Her comment began to thaw the chill that had formed like a block of ice, deep inside Clara's gut, at Brock's presence then at the implication of his words.

She felt more than saw Fitz return, carrying his clean, masculine scent with him. He settled himself right next to her on the loveseat, so close that she could feel his heat through their clothing, and it warmed her to her bones. He wrapped one arm around her and covered her hand with his.

"Baby, I am so deeply sorry. The police should be here any moment, and Mac is making sure Brock won't go anywhere in the meantime."

Lana rose, her white dress shimmering like a waterfall in the warm lighting. "I'll go wait out front, so they know where to go when they come in."

Fitz nodded at his sister, a small smile touching his mouth. "Thanks, Lana. I really appreciate it." Lana walked, with deliberate speed, toward the front entrance.

Clara was happy to see the beginnings of trust rebuilding between brother and sister, in spite of the nearly crushing guilt she was now feeling.

"Fitz, I'm the one who should be sorry. I ruined your party with my past…gosh, just like I feared I might."

Fitz's answer was instant and fierce. "My God, honey, *no*. You didn't ruin anything. I hate that you had to see that asshole again, and even be in his presence, but I can't be sorry that we know that he was behind all the weird accidents you had at your cabin. Who could have imagined he would act like that…? I stand by my comment that he was an idiot not to know what he had with you."

"But this event—this charity—is so important to you," she answered.

She wouldn't have thought it was possible, but he moved even closer and tipped her head to look at him with one warm, callused finger.

"It *is* important, Clara, but never more important than you. Don't you know that you're my world? You and Hope?" Fitz's voice cracked with the force of his emotion.

Clara wanted so badly to believe, but her heart felt bruised and uncertain. "Are you sure? I was hoping…but then, even when I try to, it doesn't seem like I fit so well into your world." Her eyes stung with tears.

"My world is wherever you and Hope are, and I can prove it."

She crinkled her eyebrows, wondering what he was talking about, but then he dropped down to kneel on the floor in front of her and she huffed out a breath of surprised understanding. As if in a dream, she heard him continue. His blue eyes held hers, and even though they were in a crowded ballroom, it felt like it was only the two of them. No one else mattered.

"Clara, I think I loved you from the moment I opened my eyes to see you, kneeling over me, looking so worried and beautiful. Just like you look now, as a matter of fact. Don't worry, honey. I'm not crazy, just crazy for *you*. I didn't know it then, but you were going to change my life." He smiled, and she couldn't help but smile back, which seemed to encourage him.

"You're amazing, and I don't think I'll ever deserve you, but I know that I can't imagine living without you and our beautiful daughter ever again. You're my home, whether we're together on my family's estate or in a little cabin in the woods—or anywhere else you want to be. Wherever you choose, baby, that's the only place I want to be."

Her eyes stung with tears at the sincerity she heard, and at the enormity of his offer. Fitz would let her choose, and more than that, he was giving up his family, along with all its influence and wealth, for her.

"Will you make me the happiest and luckiest of men by agreeing to be my wife? And letting me officially adopt Hope?"

Fitz's heart and soul were bared to her gaze, right there in his eyes, and she saw what it had cost him to risk everything by proposing to her when she might refuse. He held out a small, velvet box that looked like an antique—a box he had obviously been carrying all evening. He opened it, revealing a gorgeous, classic emerald ring.

"It was my grandmother's," he explained, answering her unspoken question.

She couldn't stand to leave him in suspense, especially since she'd already made up her mind before he'd said a word, before they'd left the house that evening.

"I love you, too," she managed to say in voice thick with tears. "I never want to be away from you again, either, and I'm sorry for ever thinking that I could. You're my Fitz, my Colin, my everything, no matter where we are…always."

Fitz's eyes were shiny with tears and filled with love…for her.

Her vision grew a little misty as well. "I'll marry you. *Of course* I'll marry you, and you and Hope and I will be an official family, but on one condition."

Fitz's face, which had been so overjoyed, now held a hint of wariness, but he still answered without missing a beat. "*Anything*, honey."

She tugged up on his hands, and he obliged her by sitting again on the loveseat where she could look right into his eyes. "I want to spend at least two weeks at the cabin every year, so we never forget what's most important—each other, family."

Fitz's relief was obvious, and amusement followed swiftly. "Agreed. Most happily." Without warning, he crushed her to him and kissed her—a deep, long, passionate kiss of love and longing, hope and belonging. "You're so beautiful, Clara Belle," he whispered. "Let's get out of here, baby."

"What about the police?" Clara asked.

Fitz stiffened, and his anger was unmistakable. "I'm sure that they'll have questions, but Mac will take the front line to give you a little rest before we have to answer them. Damn it, just thinking about what he could have done—"

"But he didn't," Clara finished, rubbing her fingers soothingly over his newly buzzed hair, then stroking down his cheek. "Take me away, then, Lieutenant Lover," she teased, and it lightened the moment, as she'd hoped.

Clara barely heard Drew and Lana's goodbyes as Fitz hurried her past them to the car. They'd hardly shut the doors before he reached for her and kissed her again, pulling her onto his lap and tangling his fingers in her hair as if he couldn't ever touch or kiss her enough.

"I never knew it could be like this, honey, and you make me so happy," he groaned. "I'm so damn glad you're mine."

She smiled against his mouth. "And you're mine... always, Fitz."

Want to see more from this author?
Here's a taster for you to enjoy!

Minne-sorta Falling in Love:
Mac of All Trades
Aurora Russell

Coming September 2022

Excerpt

"I have to admit that I'm impressed by how well you handled all the questions from the police about Brock Templeton," Lana said begrudgingly. Joe 'Mac' MacKenzie was already much too cocky, and his ego hardly needed any stroking. Watching him with the officers, though, had been like watching a master. She could easily see how he'd earned so many promotions and honors as a Navy pilot.

He shrugged, not taking his hands off the wheel, but the small smile he gave — *and why couldn't he be a little less handsome?* — was self-satisfied. "It's the accent," he answered, really laying it on thick. "Like my daddy said, a Southern man tells the best jokes and is always welcome at any dinner table or gatherin'."

She snorted, and not the usual elegant sniff that sometimes escaped, but a full-on nasal rattling noise. "You sound like Tom Hanks's cousin from the deeper South — like, the Mariana's Trench of Alabama."

"Oh, no, ma'am, not Alabama — perish the thought! My family's pure Georgia. How did you guess I was from Mariana's Trench, though?" he teased. "My granddaddy was mayor of Mariana's Trench, as a matter of fact."

She raised one skeptical eyebrow. "Matter of fact, *eh*?"

Her heart felt like it beat double-time at Mac's charming grin, flashing like the Cheshire Cat's as it was lit periodically by the streetlights they passed. *Lana Fitzhugh, you of all people know better than to get your head turned by a handsome, charming man*, she scolded herself. He'd shown himself to be overbearing, jealous and possessive when he'd fired one of the caterers on the spot earlier in the evening without even consulting her. *But you didn't disagree with his decision*, the annoyingly honest voice in the back of her head forced her to acknowledge. The caterer had actually been making her uncomfortable, but it had been *her* problem to deal with, not Mac's.

"Would I lie to such a stunning creature? You wound me, ma'am, straight to the core." He pretended to be hit by a bolt to the heart, and she couldn't help the burble of laughter that she tried to stifle. He was just so ridiculous. He was smart, funny and seemed truly dedicated to helping other men and women who'd recently left the service. Several times over the past few weeks as she'd worked closely with him to plan that night's fundraiser, she'd found herself liking him in spite of her better judgment.

The party had been an unqualified success for the worthy veteran's charity that Mac and Fitz, her second-oldest brother, had become very involved with. *Well*, she mentally amended, *it was practically perfect until Brock Templeton, Fitz's fiancée's ex-boyfriend, made a scene*, *insulted Clara and drunkenly confessed to trying to cause her to 'accidentally' lose their baby.* Brock had clammed up when they'd gotten to the police station, but thank goodness, Mac had already recorded everything on his phone.

"I know that Fitz and Clara will really appreciate your getting the police to agree to take their statements tomorrow. They don't like to leave baby Hope for too long," she answered, sobered by the recollection of the night's events.

"I'm certain they've checked in on Miss Hope, but I do believe they may be doing some, uh, private celebrating of their engagement, too—or at least, on behalf of lonely single dudes everywhere, I *hope* they are. It's not every day that a man gets the woman he loves to agree to marry him." Mac's voice was light, but there was something sad behind his tone, just below the surface.

"No...no, it's not," she agreed, snapping her mouth shut when she realized she sounded wistful. She had plenty to be grateful for, especially now that Fitz had returned to their lives, bringing the lovely Clara and Hope, shaking up the household and breaking their oldest brother, Drew, and Lana herself out of the cold, boring routines they'd been falling into.

"Clara is just lovely—and Hope, too. I couldn't be happier for them," she enthused, perhaps a bit too heartily.

Mac quirked one side of his mouth up in a wry smile. "You've convinced me...but are you sure you've convinced yourself?"

His insight surprised her.

"I suppose you're right...but please don't think it's about Clara, because she really is wonderful. I truly am happy for them." She paused, forcing herself to be truthful. "Maybe a little envious, too. A long time ago — *God*, when I was so young and arrogant, self-assured to the point of naiveté and convinced of my own completely irresistible self — I made some really awful decisions."

If he'd said anything, she probably wouldn't have continued, but he remained silent, waiting.

"I ended up with a badly trampled heart — let's call it pulverized instead of broken — and it cost me my best friend and years of my relationship with Fitz, too." Suddenly uncomfortable with just how much she'd revealed, she gave a weak laugh. "I'm sorry I said that... *burdened* you with that. You didn't ask for my life story."

Mac touched his hand to her thigh for an instant before returning it to make a hard turn with the steering wheel. "Whatever happened, it sounds like you learned a lot from it, although I am sorry it sounds like it caused you so much pain," he replied in a low, earnest voice, so different from the light, teasing tones he usually used with her. "And, Lana, nothing you could ever tell me would be a burden," he finished, clearing his throat. She wondered if he was equally uncomfortable with what he'd revealed.

Taking pity on him, she deliberately lightened the tone. "I bet you say that to all the young debutantes," she answered. "Does it ever work?"

Mac's laughter was a surprised bark. "*Touché*, Miss Fitzhugh. It might shock you to learn that I have, indeed, known my fair share of debutantes, including my two sisters."

"Now, that *is* unexpected," she agreed, although now that she pictured it, she could definitely see Mac all dressed up in a gray afternoon suit, flirting shamelessly and fetching lemonade for some pretty young thing. "Does that mean you can dance? You never asked me once tonight."

They stopped at a signal so that his face was half in the light and half out, but the expression on the half she could see was distant. The silence between them became thick and uncomfortable. Lana knew she must have mis-stepped, but she wasn't certain how.

"I don't think I can dance anymore—or at least not like I used to," he answered at last, his voice gruff. "I lost my right leg below the knee about eighteen months ago now."

Lana sucked in a sharp breath. She'd known Mac and Fitz had met in a military hospital, and she'd noticed that Mac walked with a limp, but she'd never wanted to pry, figuring that Mac would tell her about his injury if he wanted her to know. She'd never imagined he'd lost part of his leg entirely.

"Horrified? Tempted to feel sorry for me?" Mac sounded defensive. "I've had to deal with just about every type of reaction."

She touched his shoulder gently. "Nope, just surprised, since I didn't know," she answered quietly. "I can't even begin to understand how difficult recovering from an injury like that would be, and I admire your charity work even more now."

The enclosed space of the small front seat of the car felt suddenly intimate, especially so late at night, as if the two of them might be the only people awake in the city—or maybe in the world.

They pulled onto the long driveway—well, really a small, private lane—that led to the main house of her family's compound—Fitzhugh's Folly, as it was widely known, given how outrageously expensive and ostentatious it had been when her grandfather, Pat, had built it.

Tonight, it looked cavernous and dark...forlorn. *Or maybe that's just me*, Lana thought, but recognizing the source of her melancholy didn't make her feel better. Her oldest brother, Drew, had opted to stay at his high-rise apartment downtown to save time before his morning meeting. Her grandfather and Roger, who was ostensibly their butler but who was really a member of the family, along with being her grandfather's long-time companion and probably his closest friend, had gone to bed early, so the lights had likely been out in their wing since ten o'clock or so.

Fitz and Clara were staying in the large, separate guest house — which was actually the original house on the property — so Lana would be alone in the North wing of the main house. She should have been comfortable with it — in fact, she *was* very used to it, since at least three or four nights a week she had the mansion practically to herself, with its multitude of bedrooms, sitting rooms and other various spaces for practically every conceivable purpose. She often relished the solitude, after needing to be 'on' for so much of her charity work, which was no easy feat for a natural introvert who would have been happy just reading and drinking tea. Tonight, though, she felt a pang of loneliness.

Before she knew it, they'd pulled up to her front doors. They were tall, made from a thick, dark wood, and the whole impressive entryway looked forbidding, shrouded in darkness.

"They don't leave the front lights on for you?" Mac asked, breaking the silence and some of the tension.

Lana wished they did, but they weren't that kind of family. "I often get home late, and my grandfather is surprisingly frugal, so..." She shrugged, looking away. "I'm accustomed to it." She could feel Mac's gaze, but she refused to turn toward him. "I go in the side door, anyway."

Before she could tell him not to, Mac had gotten out of the car and come around to open her door, offering her his arm. He still looked impossibly handsome in the fading moonlight. It was so cold at the tail end of mid-November that his breath puffed out of his mouth in white clouds, but he looked unruffled in his pristine dress uniform.

"Let me walk you there?" he asked. When she hesitated, with one leg on the ground and one still in the car, he spoke again. "So I'm certain you're safe."

With a swift bolt of comprehension, Lana realized he must be doing this — ensuring her safety — for Fitz, as a favor to her brother, which made total sense. They hadn't totally repaired their relationship as brother and sister, since that would take a long time, but they'd made some good headway, and Fitz had always been protective of her when they had been younger. *So why do I feel so disappointed?* she wondered.

"Since you insist," she agreed, unable to keep the snap of annoyance from her voice entirely. Still, holding onto Mac's solid, warm arm, inhaling his distinctive scent, so smooth and comforting, like masculine soap and cinnamon and detergent, she wasn't sorry not to be alone. No…it was more than that. She wasn't sorry that Mac was the specific man she walked with.

Across the lawn, she saw a light come on in the guest house, which she recognized was in baby Hope's room. Silhouetted on the shades, she saw a curvy woman's figure rocking a child, and a larger outline as a man came up behind her, enveloping them in his shadow with a hug and leading them away from the window. The peace and serenity of the domestic scene, along with recollections of the love that she'd seen on their faces every time Fitz and Clara looked at each other and at tiny, perfect Hope, made her heart hurt, because she knew she would never have anything like it—and didn't deserve it, anyway. Tears filled her eyes. As their steps slowed when they neared the side entrance to her area of the house, she kept her face averted from Mac so he wouldn't see.

"I'm here safely, so you can report back to Fitz that you did your duty," she answered, more coldly than she'd intended.

"Hey, now," Mac answered, turning toward her in front of the side steps and urging her chin up with one strong but gentle finger so he could look at her face. "I never do anything I don't want to do—not anymore, in any case—and I wanted to see you to your door safely for myself, so *I* wouldn't worry." He studied her, and she had the uncomfortable sensation that he saw much more than she'd wanted. "Are those tears, sugar?"

"No," she denied in a thick voice, but her body immediately betrayed her as two droplets fell from her lashes and traced icy paths down her cheeks.

"Oh, darlin', I'm sorry. Not quite sure what I did or said, but I never meant to make you cry," he murmured in a deep, sincere voice, and Lana thought that she could have forgiven him just about anything, if there'd been something to forgive.

"It's not you," she answered. "It's just that I feel so...*alone* sometimes, you know?" she admitted.

"God, yes," he replied, with feeling. He wrapped his arms around her and pulled her close into his body, so tightly that something he had pinned to his uniform pressed into her cheek. In spite of the tiny prick of pain, she felt safer and warmer than she had for a long, long while. "You're not alone now, Lana."

She tipped her head back, and she wasn't sure whether she pushed up toward him first or he lowered his head, but somehow he closed his mouth over hers and it was sublime. At first, his lips were gentle—surprisingly soft for such a brave, tough ex-military pilot—but when she moaned, he deepened the kiss, and she savored his spicy taste, a little like the coffee they'd drunk at the police station but mostly just his own unique flavor.

She pushed herself against him, feeling his hardness rise, thick and long, against her stomach, and he tangled his hands into her up-do, dislodging bobby pins, which made tiny metallic pings as they landed on the steps. He caressed her tongue with his, claiming her mouth in bold strokes until her nipples tightened against his chest as she imagined how he would claim her with other parts of his body.

When he finally raised his mouth from hers, his breathing harsh and uneven, she noticed they must have walked together right up to the wall of the house, and her back was cold against the bricks. The rapid puffs of her breath mingled with the clouds of his, and he leaned his forehead against hers.

"I'm sorry... I got a little carried away," Mac said, and they still stood so close that she could feel the quick rise and fall of his chest against her breasts.

"No, no...I was just as into it, maybe more," she said, then flushed with embarrassment. "I didn't mean...well, you know, I'm sure you could tell that I was enjoying it, but of course we shouldn't have done that."

Mac took a step back. "What do you mean?"

Lana bit her lip, feeling like she wished the ground would swallow her up. Where was some handy quicksand when you needed it?

"Well, like you said, I'm sorry, too."

Mac shook his head. "No, darlin', I'm not sorry it happened…only sorry we went so fast."

When she looked up into his face, so handsome, perfectly formed with strong lines and eyes that she couldn't make out clearly right now in the low light but that she knew were a startling deep green and probably blazing with emotion, she wished she dared to trust herself again with a good man, a kind man, a true friend like Mac. Being with someone like him wasn't in the cards for her, though. That kind of man wanted more than she could give — more than she was capable of giving anymore.

She put her hand on his chest. "Mac, there can't be anything more between us. I can't be with someone like you." She tried to be gentle, but she rushed her words as thick tears rose in her throat.

Mac took another step back, breaking all contact between them. "Someone like me, huh? Why did I think you were different?" His voice was hollow, resigned…but the tone was underlaid with hurt.

"That's not —" she started to explain, but he cut her off.

"You know what, Lana? Don't say anything you might regret. I'll stay away from you and you can stay away from me from now on, but no matter what, we'll still have to see each other sometimes, and I don't want it to be any worse than it has to be."

Lana felt as if he'd slapped her, but she forgave him for lashing out. He didn't understand but explaining might make it more painful. As Fitz's closest friend, he *was* bound to cross her path in the future at important events.

"If that's what you want," she agreed, her voice low and sad.

"Does it matter what I want?" Mac's laugh was mirthless, and he started to turn away. "No, hold on. I'm gonna say one more thing first, because I vowed that if I ever started to feel for someone again, that I would say the words out loud—not leave confusion or doubt."

Lana braced herself for whatever he was going to say, but his words were more surprising for their tenderness than anything else.

"It sounds like we don't feel the same way and maybe you won't thank me for saying this, but no matter how you feel, I care about you. I was beginnin' to think I might be able to care pretty deeply and that maybe you could, too."

She winced at the raw tone of his voice.

"That doesn't change overnight. Truth is, for a man like me, that doesn't really change, *period*. So if you're ever in trouble, or hurting—no matter everything we said tonight—you can call me and I'll be there. That's it."

His offer stunned her, and letting him turn around and walk away, back into the darkness that was beginning to streak gray with the first light of the coming dawn, was one of the worst things she'd ever forced herself to do. He'd be better off without her, though. She knew it, and he'd recognize it, too, in time.

She'd thought her sad, shredded heart was incapable of feeling anything anymore, but now she learned—too late—that she must have been mistaken. If it had truly been destroyed, it couldn't hurt so darn bad now. She hurried inside the massive house, her steps echoing off the walls and floors of the empty rooms, and cried for everything that might have been.

About the Author

Aurora is originally from the frozen tundra of the upper-Midwest (ok, not frozen all the time!) but now loves living in New England with her real-life hero/husband, two wonderfully silly sons, and one of the most extraordinary cats she has ever had the pleasure to meet. But she still goes back to the Midwest to visit, just never in January.

She doesn't remember a time that she didn't love to read, and has been writing stories since she learned how to hold a pencil. She has always liked the romantic scenes best in every book, story, and movie, so one day she decided to try her hand at writing her own romantic fiction, which changed her life in all the best ways.

Aurora loves to hear from readers. You can find her contact information, website details and author profile page at https://www.totallybound.com

TOTALLY BOUND

Home of Erotic Romance

Sign up for our newsletter and find out about all our romance book releases, eBook sales and promotions, sneak peeks and FREE romance books!